USA TODAY bestselling author **Heidi Rice** lives in London, England. She is married with two teenage sons—which gives her rather too much of an insight into the male psyche—and also works as a film journalist. She adores her job, which involves getting swept up in a world of high emotions; sensual excitement; funny, feisty women; sexy, tortured men; and glamorous locations where laundry doesn't exist. Once she turns off her computer, she often does chores—usually involving laundry!

Books by Heidi Rice

Harlequin Presents

Bound by Their Scandalous Baby
Claimed for the Desert Prince's Heir
A Forbidden Night with the Housekeeper
Innocent's Desert Wedding Contract

One Night with Consequences

Carrying the Sheikh's Baby

Passion in Paradise

My Shocking Monte Carlo Confession

The Christmas Princess Swap

The Royal Pregnancy Test

Visit the Author Profile page
at Harlequin.com for more titles.

To Daisy

I love you, and your little dog, too!

H x

Heidi Rice

———

ONE WILD NIGHT WITH
HER ENEMY

HARLEQUIN®
PRESENTS®

ISBN-13: 978-1-335-56879-3

One Wild Night with Her Enemy

Copyright © 2021 by Heidi Rice

This edition published by arrangement with Harlequin Books S.A.

For questions and comments about the quality of this book, please contact us at CustomerService@Harlequin.com.

Harlequin Enterprises ULC
22 Adelaide St. West, 40th Floor
Toronto, Ontario M5H 4E3, Canada
www.Harlequin.com

Printed in U.S.A.

"My seaplane's docked here. I can call you a cab back to your hotel, or you can come with me to Sunrise Island tonight."

Luke ran his thumb down the side of her face, the whisper of sensation intensifying the longing now charging through her veins. "One night. And I'll bring you back tomorrow morning."

The implication was clear. This didn't mean anything more than slaking this raw, shocking need, which had sprung from nowhere. Cassie stifled the foolish sting of disappointment and whispered, "I've never done anything like this before."

"Like what?" he asked.

Have a one-night hookup... Or any hookup at all for that matter.

The obvious answer seemed too compromising, and embarrassing.

Would he change his mind if he knew she had no experience?

"I've never done something so spontaneous," she said, settling for a less revealing answer, which was no less true.

He chuckled, that low husky laugh she had begun to adore. "Then you're way overdue, *cher.*"

Hot Summer Nights with a Billionaire

One summer to ignite passion!

When Cassie borrows a show-stopping dress from her roommate, Aisling, for a business trip, she has no idea of the consequences! She's supposed to be researching her boss's rival, Luke Broussard—*not* on his private island...in his bed!

Back in London, Aisling is stepping out of her comfort zone, too—by stepping in as PA to Cassie's very sexy boss, Zachary Temple!

Check out both stories in this sparkling duet.

Read Cassie's story in
One Wild Night with Her Enemy by Heidi Rice
Available now!

Catch Aisling's story in
The Flaw in His Red-Hot Revenge by Abby Green
Coming soon!

PROLOGUE

'YOU CANNOT BE SERIOUS, Ashling! I can see my nipples in this thing. And it feels far too…'

Dangerous? Exciting?

Cassandra James cut off the errant thought. The dress her flatmate and BFF Ashling Doyle had sourced for her to wear to an *über*-hip celebrity wedding in San Francisco, in exactly fourteen hours' time, was not dangerous, or exciting, it was—well, frankly, it was indecent.

Her boss, Zachary Temple, had asked her to go to the wedding to check out Luke Broussard of Broussard Tech, in what Temple had referred to as 'his natural habitat', before kicking off a two-week trip to the West Coast to scope out investment prospects for Temple Corp in the buoyant US technology market.

As Temple's trusted executive assistant, Cassie had done some of the groundwork before on his investment decisions—crunching numbers and rigorously fact-checking industry credentials when she wasn't doing all the usual admin her job entailed… She enjoyed the rare chance to branch out, and she knew she'd impressed Temple with her work and her recommendations.

He'd given her this assignment after she'd voiced her concerns about Broussard's background check. And it was a huge opportunity to stop being a glorified gopher and move up the corporate ladder. The only problem was that up till now she'd always worked in the comfort of Temple Corp's HQ in London, not by attending a glittering society event an ocean away, full of super-cool people.

She hadn't told Temple of her concerns when he'd given her the assignment out of the blue, because it would have made her look and feel pathetic. And it was only a wedding, for goodness' sake.

Plus, she had been right to suggest Broussard might need closer inspection. She hadn't been able to discover anything about his origins or his background online… It was almost as if the details had been deliberately erased. The extensive internet research she'd done on him had offered up a ton of glowing reviews on the stratospheric rise of his company from innovative start-up to global player in less than a decade, and a few furtively snapped paparazzi shots of Broussard himself with an assortment of beautiful women on his arm. But not a lot else…

Going to San Francisco to see if she could discover more about him in person made sense. And asking Ashling—who had a quirky eye for fashion and had always been the coolest person Cassie knew—to source a dress for the wedding had seemed like the perfect solution to calm any residual nerves…

But then Ashling had produced this glittering gold creation which clung intimately to every one of Cassie's curves.

'You can't wear a bra with that dress, Cass,' Ashling reiterated, standing at Cassie's shoulder. 'It'll ruin the shape.' She stepped back, the sparkle in her blue eyes taking on an assessing gleam. 'You look amazing.'

'Seriously, Ash? I can feel my boobs swaying.' Cassie placed her hands on her breasts for emphasis—and some much-needed support.

Ashling's lips pursed into an adorable pout, which Cassie knew her friend could use like a lethal weapon—as she had so often when they were growing up together. As the daughter of their housekeeper, Ashling had quickly become Cassie's ally and her best friend. Someone who could tempt her into the best adventures and out of the shell created by her father's disapproval.

Cassie had always adored her childhood friend for her free spirit. But she was loving that free spirit a lot less at the moment. Because she did not have the time—or the talent—to find an alternative dress before the car arrived to take her to Heathrow.

'If you wear a bra with that dress you'll be committing a major fashion faux pas,' Ashling said, still pouting—and totally missing the point. 'This dress is perfect for a fancy celebrity wedding in San Francisco…'

Ashling paused as the colour flared in Cassie's cheeks. And the anxiety Cassie had kept ruthlessly at bay ever since Temple had dropped his bombshell so casually about this trip threatened to strangle her.

'Cass, what's wrong?' her friend said, her voice rich with concern.

'Nothing,' she said automatically. But then she breathed in. *Damn*. If she couldn't tell Ashling how she really felt, who could she tell? 'I just do not want to go to this thing.'

There—she'd said it.

'Why?' Ashling asked.

Cassie frowned. 'Lavish social events aren't my forte.'

She could still remember the time her father had asked her to host an important soirée when she was eighteen. It had felt like a test—a test she'd been desperate to pass and had comprehensively failed. He'd never asked her again.

'And, anyway, Temple's not sending me to socialise. He wants me to check out a tech entrepreneur called Luke Broussard while I'm at the wedding.' Cassie stared at herself in the mirror again. 'And this dress feels like too much.'

Ashling's blue eyes softened, and the fierce solidarity Cassie had relied on so heavily throughout her childhood was ringing in her voice when her friend banded her arms around her waist and rested her chin on Cassie's shoulder. 'It's not. It's gorgeous. You look like a sex goddess. Which makes it the perfect dress to wear to conduct some industrial espionage. You'll dazzle this Luke dude into giving up all his secrets while he's ripping it off you in a passionate frenzy.'

Cassie gulped as she recalled the pictures of Luke Broussard which she'd pored over maybe a bit too forensically. A slightly hysterical laugh slipped out as she conjured up the far too vivid image of Luke Broussard's large hands tearing glittering gold *lamé*.

'"Passionate" is not what I'm looking for,' she announced, as firmly as she could, while fighting to ignore the weight now sinking into her abdomen.

Good grief, trust Ashling to put that totally inappropriate thought into my head.

'And this trip is not about industrial espionage. I'm just going to help Temple suss out some potential investment opportunities and I don't want to mess it up. I need to blend in with the crowd,' Cassie added, pretty sure that Ash's dress choice was going to make her stick out like a sore thumb. Albeit a gold-plated one.

Ashling grinned and spread out her arms as if she were introducing Cassie to a crowd of admiring onlookers. 'Then my work here is done.'

Cassie sent Ashling what she hoped was a stern look, but then her phone buzzed and her worries about the dress got hit by a more immediate problem as a message from her assistant Gwen popped up.

Cassie, so sorry, my back's playing up. Won't be able to do the tux pick-up today.

Cassie swore softly under her breath.

'What is it?' Ash asked.

Cassie lifted her head to find her friend sending her a quizzical look. 'Ash, could you do me a humungous favour?'

'Of course—what's the favour?' Ash said, and Cassie wanted to kiss her despite the dress debacle.

'Could you pick up Temple's tuxedo from the dry cleaners this afternoon and deliver it to his place in Mayfair by six? He has a big event tonight and Gwen's just bailed on me. I can text you his address on the way to the airport,' she said, as she frantically tried to find the zip on the dress.

'Can't he get his own tuxedo?' Ash replied, surprising Cassie.

'Um…no. And I need someone I can trust to pick it up for him.'

Ash wasn't always super-reliable, but if she said she'd do something she would. And she would go to the wall for Cassie, so surely…?

'Seriously? There isn't anyone else you could ask?' Ash said.

'Not at such short notice,' Cassie said, confused by Ash's continued resistance—her friend was usually so helpful. 'Ash, what's the problem?'

As far as she knew Ash had never met Temple, and she'd never detected any animosity from her friend before about her boss. That said, they were total opposites. Because Ash was warm and sweet and slightly kooky, and Temple… Well, Temple so *wasn't*. But…

'It's fine. I'll do it.' Her friend cut through Cassie's thoughts, bending her head to work on the dress zip. 'I'm just not keen on being a billionaire's handmaiden, that's all. It's nothing personal.'

'Okay...' Cassie studied her friend a moment longer. Was Ash blushing? 'Are you sure?'

Ashling rolled her eyes so hard Cassie was surprised she didn't dislocate her eyeballs. 'Of course. My yoga class finishes at three-thirty. I'll have plenty of time.'

'Right... Great...' Cassie said as her friend eased down the zip.

The dress slipped over her hips, triggering a rush of sensation. She dived for the T-shirt she'd left on the bed, far too aware of a strange feeling of exposure... And vulnerability?

What was with *that*?

Okay, so she was technically still a virgin—thanks to a couple of really lacklustre dates at university—but she was hardly a complete novice. She'd kissed her fair share of guys. And the only reason she'd never gone the whole way was because her career had always been more important than her sex-life.

Was that where her concerns about this event really came from?

She pulled the T-shirt over her head.

No, that couldn't be it. Maybe she wasn't that comfortable without her professional armour firmly in place, but she had never been intimidated by men like Broussard—rich, powerful men—because she'd spent the last three years of her life working in close proximity to Temple.

'Now, you need to pack this dress and get going, if you're going to make your flight.' Ash scooped the dress off the floor. 'And try to enjoy your trip, even if it is work. There's no harm mixing business with pleasure occasionally.'

That trickle of anxiety returned at Ashling's teasing remark—and joined the swelling in Cassie's throat and a few more disconcerting parts of her anatomy.

No more overthinking, Cassie. It's just a job.

But the gold *lamé* still felt dangerous—and exciting—as she folded the dress into her suitcase.

CHAPTER ONE

You were right about the dress, Ash. I'm not even the most naked woman here... But what happened with the tux? You had one job, Ash!!

LUKE BROUSSARD TOOK another sip from his beer and continued to watch the woman standing on the opposite side of the arbour as she finished texting, switched off her phone and tucked it back in her purse. Her gold dress shimmered in the dusky orange light as the sun sank into San Francisco Bay, accentuating her high breasts and slender neck.

He'd spotted her twenty minutes ago, busy fending off all the eligible heterosexual bachelors, as soon as he'd arrived at this wedding in the Botanical Gardens. That stunning dress and the even more stunning figure it displayed had been turning heads ever since.

But it wasn't her body which had snagged *his* attention. Not entirely, anyway.

He sipped the cold brew again, to douse the low-grade fire in his pants which was calling him a liar.

Nah, the thing that had *really* intrigued him was the fact that he didn't recognise her. And he was pretty sure he knew all the available women on the West Coast scene, because he'd either dated them or they'd hit on him.

Who the heck is she?

At first he'd wondered if she'd crashed the event. He'd crashed enough of these things himself, when he'd been starting out and trying to get funding for Broussard Tech's first prototypes, to make the thought fire his imagination and his libido.

As he'd observed her, though, he'd discarded that idea. She looked way too elegant and aloof to be here without an invitation.

Which only made her more fascinating.

Her unattainable, ethereal beauty reminded him of the girls he'd never been good enough for in high school. The rich, fancy, privileged girls from the *right* side of the tracks who had been eager to make out with him after-hours on a game night, but had ignored him the next day in class because he'd lived in a trailer park, had a deadbeat for a father, worked two jobs and still hadn't been able to afford the latest high-tops.

Those memories amused him now he was worth billions and change.

But could that explain why the woman in gold had captured his attention? Did she represent a chance to relive those old high school humiliations and win? No woman was unattainable to him now. Not even one as stunning as her.

He gulped his beer as he noticed her chewing her bottom lip. Maybe she wasn't as aloof and composed as she seemed. He continued to study her. She actually looked kind of tense. Not aloof so much as uncomfortable.

Interesting. He hated these types of events, too.

He would never usually attend something like this, because if there was one thing he hated more than being on display, it was being on display in a monkey suit.

He tugged at his shirt collar and dragged off the tie which had been strangling him ever since the happy couple had said their vows five minutes ago. He shoved the tie in his pocket. If the two grooms hadn't once saved him from complete social isolation in college he wouldn't have come to this event either, but now he was here he was glad he hadn't dodged it. And not just because hearing Matt and Remy make their vows had been so touching.

When was the last time a woman had demanded his attention?

The mystery lady in gold stopped chewing her lip to chew the edge of her thumbnail, then stiffened. She drew her hand down to clutch the purse resting on her hip.

Another guy approached her. Luke tensed.

Back off, buddy, she's mine.

The possessive thought came out of left field. *Not cool.*

He'd stopped letting his libido make decisions for him ever since those nights under the bleachers. These days he had his security team check out anyone he was considering dating to ensure he didn't hook up with women who were more interested in his platinum credit rating than his make-out skills.

The only problem was, that had taken all the fun out of the chase.

His heartrate spiked as the mystery girl gave the guy—whom he recognised as a rival tech company's CEO—the brush-off. For the first time in a long time he felt the heady adrenaline rush which meant he wanted to stop watching and start finding out more about this woman… A lot more.

He dumped his beer on the tray of a passing waiter, scooped up a couple of glasses of fancy fizz and strode past the arbour towards her.

To hell with the security check.

Whoever she was, she was the first woman to snag his interest in way too long for him to remember—which gave her considerable cachet in the jaded world of billionaire hook-ups.

Plus, there was nothing he loved more than a mystery that needed to be solved.

As he drew closer she looked directly at him, like a deer sensing the approach of a hunter. Their gazes collided and her eyes—hazelnut-brown shot through with flecks of gold that matched her dress—popped wide. With recognition or surprise or arousal, he couldn't be sure.

The shimmering gold fabric hugged the round weight of her breasts, making them look even more spectacular up close.

Is she wearing a bra?

His breath backed up in his lungs.

She really was exquisite—much more refined and beautiful than any of the girls he'd hooked up with in high school. He forced his wayward gaze back to her face. The flush of reaction—and guilty knowledge—highlighted her pale cheeks.

Arousal for sure, then. And recognition. And something else he couldn't decipher—but he would.

Lust fired through his bloodstream and hit his groin like a missile.

Well, damn...

'Hi.'

He handed her the champagne glass and gave himself a mental high-five when she took it. He wanted her more than he'd wanted any woman in a while. And before the night was over he intended to have her—after all, his make-out skills had improved considerably since high school, and he'd never had a problem getting any girl he wanted even when he'd been the boy good girls were warned to stay away from.

But first he was more interested in uncovering all the fascinating secrets lurking in those big, beautiful and guarded eyes.

'Drink up, *cher*,' he said, laying on the Cajun manners his mama had drummed into him as a kid. 'Whatever you said to Dan Carter to send him packing,' he added, clinking his glass against hers as he mentioned the CEO she'd just given the bird, metaphorically speaking, 'I salute you. The guy's an entitled jerk. I have it on good authority.'

Luke Broussard! In the flesh.

'You... You do?' Cassie spluttered, taking a gulp of the champagne the man she'd been discreetly trying to locate in the crowd had just handed to her.

'I do.'

He tapped his nose, his firm, sensual lips stretching into a grin so full of laid-back hotness she could feel the effect right down to her toes—even in the heeled sandals which had been punishing her feet for over an hour.

Funny thing… She couldn't feel the pain any more as she became fixated on that seductive smile—full of confidence, and heat, and rueful amusement…and directed squarely at her. As if they were sharing a particularly good joke.

Although that couldn't be right.

She tried to get her jet-lagged brain back into gear.

Was this actually happening? Or was she imagining it out of desperation and fatigue and the Aperol Spritz she'd chugged down too quickly as she'd struggled to relax enough to make small talk?

She'd been at the wedding for what felt like an eternity, and there had been no sign of Luke Broussard and no one who knew him had seemed willing to talk about him. But Ashling's dress choice had worked its magic—or rather its curse—because she'd been approached by a selection of increasingly pushy guys, the last of whom had asked her point-blank if she'd like to spend the night on his yacht.

She'd met enough American men in business to know they could often be staggeringly forthright, but the leer in that man's eyes had made her feel unclean.

Luke Broussard's eyes, though—a striking emerald changing to a deep forest-green around the rim of his irises—were full of something a great deal more dangerous to her peace of mind… Not to mention her breathing… Because the look in them had triggered an urge to step closer to him, to gather the hint of his clean scent—pine soap overlaid with man—and bask in the mocking approval in his expression. Which could not be good.

His husky American accent sounded different from the others she'd heard this evening too. Slower, deeper, less sharp, the soft purr brushing over her skin and making it tight and achy.

The snapped, mostly blurred shots she'd found of him on the internet hadn't done him justice. He'd seemed conventionally handsome in those pictures, but in person his features were more rugged and a great deal more breathtaking. The strong jaw, darkened with the first hint of stubble, was matched by a prominent nose and chiselled cheekbones. His left brow was rakishly bisected by a piratical scar, and his dark wavy hair looked as if he'd missed his last few appointments at the barbers.

The hint of a tattoo on his collarbone—was that barbed wire?—revealed by the open collar of his shirt, only added to the aura of raw masculinity, untamed and defiant, and as out of place in this exclusive setting as she was... But for entirely different reasons.

The shock of having him walk up to her so boldly gave way to curiosity—and that odd yearning which she'd have to examine later. *Much later.*

For goodness' sake, Cassie, say something smart and erudite. Draw him out. Don't stare at him like a dummy.

She took another sip of champagne to buy some time and think up something coherent to say. Why did this feel like a strange exotic dream—both dangerous and exciting—rather than a golden opportunity to further the interests of Temple Corp?

'I'm not sure if Mr Carter is a jerk,' she managed, having finally grasped enough of the conversation to actually participate, 'but he was certainly very forward.'

'Forward, huh?' Broussard's scarred eyebrow arched and his lips quirked as if she'd said something amusing. 'What was his pick-up line?'

'He invited me to spend the night on his yacht. Apparently it's very big.'

His lips quirked some more. 'Classy,' he murmured. 'What did you say?'

'I told him the truth—that it probably wasn't a good idea as I can get seasick on a pedalo.'

His eyes sparkled, the tantalising curl of his lips making her breath thready. What was it about his smile that made it seem dangerous and precious at the same time?

'A peda— what, now?' he asked.

'A pedalo. It's like a small paddle boat with pedals you use to propel it, usually on a boating lake...' She babbled to a stop as those beautifully sculpted lips tipped up even further at the edges.

Shut up, Cassie, why are you composing an encyclopaedia entry on pedalos for him?

'Interesting,' he said, even though they both knew what she'd just said wasn't interesting in the slightest. 'You're British, right?'

'What gave me away?' she asked, and the appreciation in his eyes added a spurt of exhilaration to the tangle of nerves in her belly.

She took another hasty sip of the champagne to calm them. It didn't work.

'The cute accent,' he said, with that dangerous gaze roaming over her face. 'And the peaches and cream complexion.'

Her peaches and cream complexion heated accordingly.

'You blush real prettily too, *cher*,' he added.

Her cheeks promptly ignited.

The sun had dipped behind the headland in the distance and a row of flaming torches was now lighting the gardens edged by a lavish arboretum—expertly planted with everything from Mesoamerican ferns to African impatiens, according to the plaques Cassie had read while trying to pluck up the courage to talk to strangers. But even in the glow of twilight Luke Broussard had to be able to see her blush. The fact that he seemed to be enjoying her gaucheness wasn't making Cassie feel any less out of her depth.

'What does that mean?' she asked, trying to steer the conversation back to neutral territory and give herself time to get her breathing back on track. *'Shar?'* she asked, struggling to pronounce the word he'd used. 'It sounds French.'

'Cher?' he said again, and she nodded. 'It's Louisiana French, or French Cajun. I'm from the bayou originally—a sleepy little town just outside Lafayette.'

It was more information than she'd been able to glean about him online, but as she tried to think of a follow-up question his emerald-green irises darkened to a rich jade.

'And *cher* is Cajun for *cherie*…which is what you call a lady when you like the way she blushes.'

'Oh,' she managed, and her next question was drowned out by the thunder of her heartbeat.

Was Luke Broussard hitting on her? It seemed so outside the realms of possibility that she didn't know what to do with the information. Other than pray it didn't send her pulse-rate any further into the red zone. Passing out would definitely not be good.

She knew she wasn't a troll, and that Ashling's dress was doing its best to advertise every single one of her assets. But right now she really wished she had a lot more sexual experience than a few unimpressive kisses at college… For example, was the heavy weight now wedged between her thighs and pulsing in time with her heartbeat normal?

She'd always assumed she wasn't a sexual person. And she had always thought she preferred it that way. Her career was all she needed, because it defined her and motivated her and gave her life meaning and purpose.

But that had been before she'd stood in the glow of firelight, inhaled the scent of salt water and rose petals and pine soap carried on the summer breeze off San Francisco Bay, and felt a strange thrill charge through her system as Luke Broussard's attention—and those playful green eyes—focussed solely on her.

She couldn't think clearly…couldn't feel anything but the prickle of sensation awakening every one of her nerve-endings…and couldn't say anything except, 'That's…very sweet.'

Broussard's brows shot up, and he barked out an astonished laugh. 'Fair warning…' His gaze darkened as he traced his fingertip over her burning cheek. 'No woman has ever accused me of being sweet, *cher.*'

The casual endearment sounded anything but sweet in his deep, husky purr, and the torturously light touch ignited the weight between her thighs.

'My name's Luke Broussard,' he said. 'Of Broussard Tech,' he added, as if there was any need—surely everyone in San Francisco knew who he was?

'I know,' she said.

'That leaves me at a disadvantage. Because I don't know who you are.'

'Cassandra James. I work for Zachary Temple at Temple Corp as his executive assistant.'

She bit her tongue the minute the words were out of her mouth. Should she have told him that? After all she was supposed to be here incognito, until Temple made a decision on her investment report's recommendations.

To her relief, he seemed unfazed by the information.

'Temple Corp, huh? I've heard of them,' he said.

She remembered he had no way of knowing yet that Temple was considering investing in his company. Her panic downgraded a notch.

Until he asked, 'So how do you know Remy and Matt?'

Anxiety kicked in as she struggled to recall the story she'd invented on her eleven-hour flight. But then something Ashling had once said to her—after they had sneaked out of her father's stultifying house one Saturday, for a day of adventure in Soho, and ended up getting interrogated by her governess—rippled through her consciousness…

'If you have to tell a lie, I've heard it's better to stick to the truth as much as possible.'

'Actually, I don't know the grooms,' she confided. 'I'm here as Temple's representative. He wanted to pay his respects, but he couldn't make it himself.'

Which wasn't actually a lie. Temple Corp *was* one of Remy Carlton and Matt Donnelly's biggest clients, because Temple always preferred to use their boutique hotels whenever he travelled, and his invitation to the wedding had been entirely genuine.

Broussard nodded, but a small frown appeared on his brow. 'That's a thing now?'

'What's a thing?' she asked, panicked again by his sceptical look. She really was not cut out for industrial espionage, however slight. It was already hard enough to keep hold of the conversation when the sensation now sprinting up her spine was turning her nipples into lethal weapons.

Please don't let him notice I'm not wearing a bra.

'Getting your executive assistant to stand in for you at social events,' Broussard supplied, then gave another of those rough chuckles which tickled her right down to her toes. 'I need to get me an executive assistant like you. I hate being sociable.'

'Are you kidding? You're a lot better at it than I am,' she said bluntly, her guilty conscience loosening her tongue.

This time he threw back his head to laugh, giving her a glimpse of the strong column of his throat and the tattoo peeking above the open collar of his shirt.

That strange bubble of exhilaration burst in her chest when that dangerous green gaze met hers again and she saw approval in his eyes.

'Has anyone ever told you you're super-cute, Cassandra?'

Efficient? Professional? Smart? Boringly conventional? Yes. Super-cute...?

'Um…no, never.'

He continued to chuckle, his playful grin

making his rugged features look almost boy-
ish. 'Have you ever been to the city before?'

'No, I've never been to Frisco before,' she
said.

'I can tell,' he said, wincing theatrically.

'How?' she asked, mesmerised all over again
by the approving look.

'If you'd ever been before you'd know what
the locals think of that nickname.'

'Frisco is bad?' she asked.

'Frisco can get you a one-way ticket to Al-
catraz. I found that out the hard way when I
moved here.'

'Good to know.' She grinned.

Were they flirting? Why had she never tried
this before? It was actually fun. And she wasn't
as horrendous at it as she had assumed.

'How about we get the hell out of here?' he
said as he lifted her now empty glass from her
numb fingers. He placed it and his own on a
wooden bench. 'Seeing as being social really
isn't our thing, I could show you the city they
don't call Frisco.'

The husky intimacy in his tone, and the intensity darkening his gaze to a rich emerald, made
it clear that the offer was loaded with all sorts
of possibilities—not one of them safe.

For a fleeting moment it occurred to her that
accepting Luke Broussard's offer would be the

perfect opportunity to find out more about him for Temple... But she knew that wasn't why she wanted to say yes.

She felt light-headed, detached from reality. Every practical and pragmatic consideration in her head was becoming soft and fuzzy and insubstantial as a heady shot of adrenaline powered through her veins.

She studied his outstretched hand—capable, tanned, scarred—and the reckless streak she hadn't even known she had shot through her like a drug.

And then she remembered what Ash had said what seemed like a million years ago in London.

'There's nothing wrong with mixing business and pleasure occasionally.'

Why not take him up on his offer? There was no reason she shouldn't enjoy herself while she found out a bit more about him. *It's just a drive.*

She raised her gaze to Luke's and had the strangest sensation that she was about to step off a cliff. But before she could second-guess herself, she placed her hand in his. 'Yes, I'd like to.'

His hand wrapped around her fingers and he lifted them to his lips. The chivalrous gesture was comprehensively contradicted by the heated purpose in his gaze when he murmured something in heavily accented French.

'Laissez les bon temps rouler.'

She had no clue what the words meant. But as he led her through the crowd the jolt of adrenaline became turbo-charged.

CHAPTER TWO

SPELLBOUND.

That's what he was.

Luke figured he probably ought to be disturbed by how much he had wanted Cassandra James to say yes. But as he placed his hand on her lower back and handed his ticket to the valet, and she shuddered violently, he found it hard to give a damn.

He hadn't discovered a thing about her except that she was British, and she worked for a British billionaire investor whom he'd heard of but didn't know much about. But that didn't stop his yearning to place his lips on the nape of her neck below her hairline and inhale her scent.

Even gilded by the dusk, that killer blush still ignited her cheeks. Cassandra James presented a challenge—a challenge he hadn't even known he wanted. She seemed unable to hide her physical response to him, and he sensed she lacked

the sexual confidence of the women he usually dated.

He had no idea why he found that so refreshing. He wasn't a guy who had ever prized hon-
esty when it came to dating—everyone had
their secrets, him most of all, and he respected
that, understood it. Sex didn't mean intimacy—
certainly not where he was concerned—but she
excited him on more than just a physical level.

The valet pulled up at the kerb, riding the vintage 955cc motorbike Luke had reconditioned
himself last winter.

Cassandra swung her head round, her golden
eyes widening to saucer-size. 'You're not serious? I can't ride that.'

He chuckled—he couldn't help it. Her
shocked expression was as hot as her slight pout
of disappointment.

'Sure you can. I have a spare helmet,' he said,
as he handed a hundred-dollar bill to the valet.

'How much change do you need, sir?' the
boy asked.

'None, kid. I'm trying to impress the lady
here.'

The boy grinned as he pocketed the cash, the
flush of pleasure on his face more than worth
the money. 'Yes, sir, and thank you, sir. That's
the biggest tip I've had all night.'

'I'll bet,' he replied. 'Working service jobs

for rich folks never tips as good as it should— am I right?'

'It does now, sir,' the boy said, still grinning as he saluted him before heading off to deal with another couple who had just arrived in the parking lot.

'That was very generous of you,' Cassandra remarked.

'Like I said, I was trying to impress you,' he replied, and her gaze was so rich with appreciation it suddenly didn't feel like a joke any more.

'You succeeded,' she said, but then she tilted her head to one side and added, 'But that's not why you did it. You enjoyed putting that smile on his face. Did you work a lot of service jobs before you founded Broussard Tech?'

It was a probing question—the kind he usually avoided answering. He never talked about his past. He also didn't much like being figured out so easily. Since when had he become so transparent? But, even so, her expression— perceptive but also impressed—had the truth coming out.

'My fair share. And my takeaway was, the richer the customer, the more invisible you become.'

'But not to you?'

He hesitated, taken aback not just by the appreciation in her voice, but by the way it made him feel. His heart pulsed too hard in his chest. He braced himself against the uncomfortable sensation.

Time to get this seduction back on track. He didn't need to impress her—he just needed to persuade her to get on the bike. Hot and giddy was what he wanted…sincere and genuine not so much.

He unbuckled the bike's saddlebag and pulled out the helmets. 'Here you go,' he said as he offered her one.

She tucked her bottom lip under her teeth, sending another jolt of heat straight through him.

'I really don't think I can… I've never ridden a motorcycle before. Isn't it dangerous?'

Yeah, but not in the way you think.

'That's all part of the rush,' he said.

She still looked unsure, her hands clasped behind her back as if she were determined not to take the bait, however much she might want to.

Inspiration struck.

'How about we try this?' he said, then plucked the pins out of her hair.

'Oh!' Her hands flew up to save her hairdo, but it was already too late, and the fragrant mass was tumbling down over her bare shoulders.

He laughed. 'How about, if you come for a

ride on my bike, I do something I've never done before, too?'

She frowned, her confused expression only making her more adorable.

'Well, I don't see how that's going to work. I bet there isn't anything you've never done.'

Smart girl.

'Not true.' He stifled a chuckle as he racked his brains to think of something that would work. 'I've never let a lady ride on my bike before. How about that?'

'Really?' she said, and he could see the astonishment in her eyes, and then the pleasure.

The reaction should have made him uncomfortable. He didn't like to give a woman the impression she was special or different, because it might lead to misunderstandings. But the truth was he'd never wanted a woman on the back of his bike before now.

He got a kick out of riding the vintage machine through the city solo whenever he was in town. He'd always been a loner. But wanting to share it with her didn't have to mean anything. He needed to kick her out of her comfort zone, so he had no problem taking a small step outside his own.

'Yeah, really,' he confirmed. 'You'll be my first passenger.'

The emotion on her face made his heartbeat uneven as he waited for her answer.

'Okay, you're on,' she said, with a determined expression which was half-excitement and half-terror. 'Give me the helmet,' she added, holding out her hand.

'Let me,' he said, scooping her chestnut locks into his fist, no longer able to resist the desire to touch her. Her hair whispered against his palm, soft and silky, but he had to let it go after he'd placed the helmet on her head, to clip the chin buckle and adjust the straps for a snug fit.

'I bet I look completely ridiculous,' she said as he put on his own helmet.

'Not at all,' he said, stifling the urge to kiss her.

He needed to take this slow. He knew anything worth having was worth working for. And Cassandra James definitely ticked that box.

The sea breeze fluttered the ends of her hair peeking out from underneath the helmet and she shivered. He shrugged out of his tux jacket and placed it over her bare shoulders. 'Here, put this on—it might get chilly.'

She wasn't a short woman, but even so his jacket engulfed her. Sadly, it covered up her magnificent breasts in that clingy material, but he forced himself not to sulk. If his luck held tonight, and their chemistry proved as strong as it seemed, he would get a much better look soon enough.

'Now I *know* I look ridiculous,' she said, rolling up the sleeves. 'But thank you.'

He climbed aboard the bike, adjusted the throttle and kick-started the engine.

She jumped and he grinned. 'Don't worry. I promise it won't bite.'

Even if I do.

'I don't even know how to mount it,' she said, all practical as she chewed off the last of her lipstick.

He had to force his gaze off her reddened bottom lip and ignore the swift kick to his gut.

Whoa, buster, no dirty thoughts while driving or you'll wipe out.

'Gather your gown up,' he said, 'and tuck it under your knees when you get seated. We don't want it snagging on anything. There's a pedal there to stand on and mount up.'

She nodded, her frown making his lust kick again. He was treated to an impressive display of long, toned thigh before she put one foot on the pedal and flung her other leg over the bike. Grasping his shoulders, she bounced up behind him.

'Hang on tight,' he said, and her slender arms banded around his waist.

Her soft breasts flattened against his back,

and the kick burned down to his crotch. Heck, he needed to get his response under control, or this ride was going to be torture.

Her helmet clicked the back of his.

'Oops, sorry,' she said. 'Are you sure you want to do this? I'm a complete novice.'

Her thighs hugged his butt, and it was all he could do not to weep.

'Positive,' he groaned.

Revving the engine, he settled his hand on her bare knee and gave it a reassuring squeeze— then he let her go, before the sizzle against his palm could add to the torture.

'Just remember to lean with me on the turns. I'll take it slow at first, until you get the hang of it. If there's a problem, yell.'

Her helmet clicked his again as she nodded.

'All set, *cher*?' he asked.

'As I'll ever be,' she yelled, above the rumble of the bike's engine.

He peeled the bike away from the kerb and heard her shocked gasp, felt her breath hot against his nape, her arms locking tighter around his waist.

The grin that split his face as they headed down the street made him wonder why the heck he hadn't thought of taking a woman for a ride on his bike before now.

'Oh, my goodness,' she said, as she clung on and he whipped around the traffic on Lincoln Way.

She tightened her grip again when he hung a left on Clayton. Her intoxicating scent mixed with the aroma of exhaust fumes and stale weed as he slowed the bike to a crawl to turn at the busy intersection into Haight Street.

'This is Haight-Ashbury!' he yelled over his shoulder. 'Where the tourists come to celebrate the Summer of Love a half-century too late.'

She giggled, the light musical sound floating on the night air. 'I feel like I should start singing a Bob Dylan song!' she shouted back.

He laughed as a shiver of sensation shot down his spine. And suddenly he knew why he'd never offered another woman a ride on his bike. Because no woman had ever captivated him the way she had.

And he hadn't even tasted her yet.

Cassie caught her breath as they entered the old hippie neighbourhood she'd read about in a guidebook on the plane but never imagined she'd have a chance to visit. Neon signs announced tattoo parlours, thrift stores and record shops, while young people spilled out of bars and restaurants dressed in a rainbow of psychedelic colours.

She absorbed every detail, astonished that

even fifty-plus years after its heyday the area could still seem edgy and exciting. But as the muscles in Luke's back tensed, she wondered if that edgy feeling came from the neighbourhood or simply from the thrill of being on Luke Broussard's bike as they rode through Haight-Ashbury.

Unlike Ashling, she'd never been the cool girl at school, or anywhere else for that matter, but she felt like the cool girl now. For one night only.

As they left the born-again hippies of Haight-Ashbury behind, the bike climbed up a hill that cut through a lush, surprisingly untamed park.

Luke slowed the bike to a stop when they reached the top and pulled off his helmet, then glanced over his shoulder. 'Hop off. I've got something to show you.'

'Okay…' She scrambled off the bike. Her pulse started to pound again as he unclipped her helmet and hooked it over the bike handles with his own.

'Where are we going?' she asked breathlessly.

'You'll see,' he said, sending her a sultry smile that had all her pheromones going haywire again. How did he *do* that? Was the guy a sex whisperer, or something? Because she'd never felt this giddy before in her entire life.

She stored the thought away as he gripped her

hand and led her past a sign that announced the park as the oldest in San Francisco. They took a path that led into the greenery.

'Should you leave the helmets on the bike like that? Won't they get stolen?' she asked, trying to find some semblance of her usual practicality.

He sent her a wry grin, as if she'd said something cute, then shrugged. 'We won't be long— but anyhow I've got others.'

Well, of course he has. The man's a billionaire, Cassie, for goodness' sake.

She tried not to fixate on the heat now running riot through her body as they reached a clearing. Then he gripped her shoulders, stood behind her and twisted her round.

'Check that out,' he said.

But her breath had already caught in her lungs.

The city was laid out before them in a carpet of lights, just starting to wink on as night fell. The staggering view spread across the dark expanse of the bay, where the white lights of the Golden Gate Bridge shone like a runway leading to the opposite shore.

'Wow!' she murmured, so awed and humbled that all she could feel was the clamour of her heartbeat in her throat. 'It's so beautiful. You must adore living here,' she managed, desperately trying to keep talking to curtail the foolish spurt of emotion.

No man had ever shown her something so magnificent. And she'd only just met him.

But why had he?

'I don't live in the city,' he said, his voice so low and husky she could feel it rippling down her back and detonating in her abdomen.

'You don't?' She twisted to see his face, illuminated by the glow from the sunset. 'But why not? It's wonderful.'

'I keep an apartment here,' he said. 'But it's not my home.'

'Where is your home?' she asked, suddenly desperate to know more about him. Much more. And knowing that it had nothing whatsoever to do with her report, because she'd stopped thinking about what Temple had asked her to do a thousand giddy heartbeats ago.

'I own an island off the Oregon coast.'

He frowned, and she got the impression he hadn't meant to tell her. But before she had a chance to worry about whether she had probed too much he took her hand again and led her back down the path they'd just climbed.

'Where are we going now?' she asked, feeling like a child—carefree and excited—which was rather ironic, given that as a child she'd always been the opposite…weighed down by worries and anxiety.

'I've got something else I think you'll enjoy,' he said, without revealing much at all.

She climbed back aboard the bike, her heartbeat skipping and jumping as he put her helmet on again. She clung to him, feeling like a pro now at leaning on the turns as they headed off into the dusk.

The bike made its way back down the hillside, winding through steep residential streets lined with San Francisco's signature bay-fronted wooden terraced houses, eventually coming to a busy two-lane road that headed through another park.

As they travelled down towards the bay, dodging cars and lorries in the snarled evening traffic, it occurred to her that she'd never allowed herself to be led anywhere before now. But as she clung to Luke's broad frame, and inhaled his clean, masculine scent, the thrill of rebellion intoxicated her.

Darkness descended as they entered a traffic tunnel, and when they emerged, her heartbeat slammed into her tonsils.

The Golden Gate Bridge towered above them, the lights from the evening traffic giving the magnificent steel structure an eerie red glow, silhouetted against the dying day. An eighteen-wheeler rumbled as they flew past it, and she stole a glance over her shoulder to see the city stacked like children's building blocks on the hillside behind them.

She sheltered behind Luke's broad back and imagined them taking flight across San Francisco Bay into the erotic dream which had blindsided her.

She wasn't Cassandra James, smart and supremely efficient executive assistant who always kept her mind on business any more. She was Cassandra James, free spirit and all-round badass.

The journey seemed to take for ever and yet no time at all. Hills shaped like sleeping giants formed the dark shoreline ahead as the suspension bridge's final supporting strut passed over their heads. They took a series of twists and turns off the main road, through manicured parks and down dark roads, to a marina covered in mist.

Luke parked the bike at the end of the point and the engine powered down as they sat in the darkness alone together, next to a small grove of palm trees. The light from a waterfront diner and the distant beat of dance music spilled into the quiet night.

Luke lifted off his helmet and hooked it over the handlebars, then twisted round to unclip hers.

'Hop down,' he said, and she suddenly wondered if she'd done something wrong, because his voice was no longer relaxed, and the playfulness had vanished from his eyes.

She had to hold on to his shoulder to get her leg over, dismounting in a tangle of gold *lamé* which only made her feel more self-conscious.

She stood shivering in his jacket, the warm weight of it reminding her of the heady scent which had engulfed her when he'd draped it over her shoulders what felt like a lifetime ago. On that other girl. The dull rule-follower who would never have got on a bike with a guy she'd just met in a million years.

She waited for him to dismount and tuck the helmets in the saddlebag, wrapping her arms around herself to stave off a shudder of inadequacy.

'Is something wrong?' she asked.

His head rose and his eyes flared. 'Yeah, actually there is.'

Then, to her utter surprise, he snagged her wrist and drew her into his arms. Suddenly she was surrounded by his warmth, his heat, the heady scent of soap and man and sea water. A pulse of need throbbed viciously as his gaze raked over her and one strong hand cradled her face.

'I want to kiss you so bad I can't think straight...'

The husky murmur was so full of need and intensity it seemed to reverberate in her sex.

'And I sure as hell can't drive.' His mouth hovered over hers and he whispered, 'Tell me you want to kiss me too, Cassandra.'

She could have said no. Maybe should have said no. But it would have been a lie.

'Yes.'

In less than a heartbeat his mouth found hers. The kiss was warm, firm, uncompromising. But where she would have expected him to be demanding he was coaxing…where she would have expected practised moves she got the thrill of desperation.

No man had ever kissed her before with such fervour, such yearning. His tongue delved deep, dancing with hers, licking and feasting, tasting and tantalising, until she was clinging to him even tighter and harder than she had as they'd flown across the bay.

Sensations bombarded her—all of them novel and intoxicating—and this time the weightless sensation in her stomach became swifter, sharper and more brutal, the longing so real and vivid it was painful.

He tore his mouth away first, then opened the lapels of his jacket to wrap his arms around her waist and draw her against his body. The insistent edge of his erection pressed into her belly through their clothing. But what would once have shocked her only excited her more.

Why did this feel so right? So new and exciting? Why did tonight feel like a night out of time? Was it the jet lag? That one Aperol Spritz and those few sips of champagne? The tour of the city? The beauty of that magnificent view and the wild ride that had followed? Or was it simply the heady feeling of being wanted so desperately and knowing she wanted with the same urgency in return?

'My seaplane's docked here. I can call you a cab back to your hotel, or you can come with me to Sunrise Island tonight.'

He ran his thumb down the side of her face and the whisper of sensation intensified the longing now charging through her veins.

'One night,' he said. 'And I'll bring you back tomorrow morning.'

The implication was clear. This didn't mean more to him than slaking this raw, shocking need which had sprung from nowhere.

She stifled the foolish sting of disappointment and whispered, 'I've never done anything like this before.'

'Like what?' he asked.

Had a one-night hook-up... Or any hook-up at all, for that matter.

The answer seemed too compromising—and

embarrassing. Would he change his mind if he knew she had no experience?

'I've never done something so spontaneous,' she said, settling for a less revealing answer which was no less true.

He chuckled, that low, husky laugh she had begun to adore.

'Then you're way overdue, *cher.*'

He lifted her hand to his mouth, spread open her fingers and bit gently into the swell of flesh beneath her thumb. The sharp nip sent sensation tearing through the last of her self-control.

Her fingertips skimmed the rough stubble on his jaw as his gaze locked on hers, dark with desire.

'If we do it right,' he said, 'the only consequence will be *bon temps*. Good times. I swear.' His gaze remained locked on hers. 'And I *know* we're gonna do it right.'

Before she could give herself too long to think—to plan or regret or become that dull rule-follower again—she nodded. 'I'd love to go with you.'

'Good,' he said, and excitement dropped like a stealth bomb into her heart.

CHAPTER THREE

'I'VE NEVER BEEN in a seaplane before!' Cassie shouted into the microphone attached to her helmet above the rumble of the plane's engines as the floats skipped over the water and the aircraft gathered speed. 'Does that mean you owe me another first?'

Luke sent her a smile. 'Nope—because I've never had a woman in this plane before either.'

She wasn't sure she believed him, but still her heartrate bumped in her chest as the plane rose from the water.

She gasped, and awe pressed against her ribs as the aircraft lifted over the Golden Gate Bridge. The plane tipped to the right, giving her a panoramic view of Oakland and San Francisco sprawled across the hillside, and she squinted to pick out the places he'd already taken her tonight.

Her heart catapulted into her throat for about the tenth time that evening. But it wasn't the amazing views as they headed out onto the open water, leaving the city lights scattered like stars behind them, that was taking her breath away.

The plane's wing lights lit Luke's frown of concentration as he handled the controls with practised efficiency.

Ashling would die of shock if she could see me now.

She choked off a slightly hysterical laugh. Luke turned, pinning her again with that intense green gaze and making her insides purr along with the plane.

'All good?' he asked.

'Wonderful,' she said.

Why had she never done anything like this before?

'The coastline is breathtaking in daylight,' he said. 'Green and rugged and untamed.'

'It looks amazing at night, too,' she said, as captivated by the man beside her as she was by the breathtaking view. 'How long does it take to get to your home?' she asked, not wanting the ride to end, but at the same time eager to kiss him again and feel his hard body against hers.

If a person was going to lose her mind for a night, she couldn't imagine a more rewarding way to do it. This was so much better than trying a contraband cigarette at boarding school, or handing in an essay three hours late, or getting your flatmate to deliver your boss's tuxedo and then discovering the fallout far too late to do anything about it.

Cassie sighed, remembering the tsunami of text messages she'd found on her phone when she'd turned it on at the airport. Tons from Gwen, from her sickbed, because she'd obviously been harassed by Temple when his tuxedo had failed to show—and one from Temple.

The tux has finally landed. Don't get your flatmate to run errands for me in future.

Ashling going AWOL on her was nothing new, but by the time Cassie had found out about the problem it had been two in the morning in the UK and there had been no point in ringing Temple to apologise profusely, or calling Ashling to give her hell for screwing up such a simple task.

So Cassie had sent Ash a text from the wedding—which her friend would get in the morning—and then switched off her phone.

Thank goodness Temple wasn't the sort to hold a grudge. But it was funny to think that ever since Luke had approached her she'd completely forgotten about Ashling's latest *ditzkrieg*.

'It'll take about an hour to get to Sunrise Island,' he barked out over the headphones.

'I… I can't wait to see it. Is there a reason why you decided to settle there?' she asked, making desperate small talk again, trying to ignore the sudden drop in her stomach.

Am I actually doing this? Travelling to a private island for a one-night stand?

The hum of the engine cut through the silence. She turned to look at him, wondering at the sudden pause in the conversation, only to realise he had the same frown on his face he'd had back in the park, when he'd told her about his island home.

'I like my privacy,' he said at last.

The rest of the journey went by in a haze of stunning night-time views as the coastline meandered north. The lights marking their way in the darkness turned from clusters into sprinkles as they journeyed into Oregon. But as Cassie stared at the coastline the buoyant sensation which had been driving her decisions all evening turned into a leaden lump in the pit of her stomach…

'I like my privacy.'

What was she actually doing? Taking him up on the offer of a one-night stand when the reason she was in San Francisco, the reason why she'd been at the wedding of his friends in the first place, wasn't as it appeared to him?

Should she tell him about Temple's interest

in investing in Broussard Tech? Wouldn't it
be hopelessly unprofessional to bring up work
now?

*Yeah, Cassie, almost as unprofessional as
climbing aboard his bike, kissing him sense-
less and agreeing to spend the night with him
on his private island?*

She blinked into the darkness, her newfound
adventurous streak tempered by a cold, harsh
dose of reality. And the spontaneous choice she
had made at the marina didn't seem quite so
simple any more.

After landing Jezebel on the sheltered east side
of Sunrise Island, Luke drove the plane into the
small secluded cove below the house. The right
float bumped against the dock as a sprinkle of
rain hit the fuselage.

'A storm's brewing.' He glanced at his passenger, who had been silent for the last half-hour
of their journey. She hadn't been the only one.

Why the heck had he invited her to Sunrise?
It had been a spur-of-the-moment decision
driven by an organ other than his brain—and
by the transparent wonder on her face when he'd
shown her the city view from his favourite spot
in Buena Vista Park.

Something about her unguarded, refreshingly
artless reaction had made him want to show her

more. And the next thing he knew he'd been heading across the bay towards Sausalito.

He had a penthouse condo in San Francisco less than a mile from the Botanical Gardens. A nice place—sleek and modern and expertly furnished at an eye-watering cost by an award-winning design team in one of the city's snootiest neighbourhoods. It was the place he always took the women he dated.

But once they'd got across the bridge the feel of her wrapped around him like superglue had driven him a little nuts, and he'd found himself taking the road to the marina where he had his plane docked.

Now her small white teeth worried at her bottom lip and the heat landed back in his lap.

Not much point trying to figure out the dumb decision to bring her to Sunrise now. With a storm brewing they were stuck here for the night, so they might as well make the most of it.

'We should probably get inside before the storm hits,' he said, unclipping his belt. 'The weather in this region can get nasty fast,' he added, unfastening her belt too, because she'd made no move to do it herself.

He turned to open the door to the aircraft and she grasped his forearm.

'Wait, Luke. I need to tell you something,' she said, and the glare from the plane's interior lights illuminated the shadows in her eyes before her gaze darted away. 'Something I should have made clear to you before I agreed to come here…'

She looked more than worried now. She looked guilty and freaked out.

The heat twisted and burned in his gut. But a kick of disgust at himself wasn't far behind, reminding him of a man he had always despised.

'Hey, Cassandra,' he said, touching her chin and lifting her head so their gazes connected. 'There's no pressure here.' His gaze dipped to take in the hint of cleavage revealed by his open jacket as he reminded himself what tonight was really all about. 'I'm not gonna lie…' He took a deep breath, deciding to give it to her straight. 'I want to explore every inch of you tonight, and make you moan and sigh and gasp a lot more…' His lips quirked as hot colour flooded into her face. 'And make you blush so hard your cheeks feel like they're on fire.'

'Actually, they already are,' she murmured.

The wry rejoinder surprised a laugh out of him in the middle of his big speech. He touched his thumb to her burning cheek and grinned, happy to be back on solid ground. Their chemistry was real and immense—this invitation wasn't about anything more than that.

'Yeah, I can tell,' he said. 'But here's the

thing,' he added. 'You don't owe me anything. There's five bedrooms in my home and no expectation that the one you sleep in tonight has to be mine. You got that?'

He forced himself to drop his hand. If she was having second thoughts he wasn't going to pressure her either way—because that would make this more than it was.

'I...' She blinked, looking taken aback. 'That's very gallant of you,' she said.

Gallant? What the...?

He choked out a laugh, relieving some of the tension snapping in his gut.

'What's so funny,' she asked, her clear-eyed pragmatism something he was becoming addicted to.

'That's another first for me,' he said. 'No woman's ever called me gallant before, either. Now you owe *me* a first.'

'Are you sure?' she asked, looking genuinely surprised. 'I suspect a lot of less gallant men *would* have expectations after flying a woman several hundred miles for a hook-up.'

Another laugh escaped on a spontaneous bark of amusement, but beneath it was a strange feeling of uneasiness. 'Yeah, I'm one hundred and one per cent positive no woman's ever even *thought* of me as gallant before,' he said.

'Then they were fools,' she said, outraged on his behalf.

'But you still owe me,' he said, to keep things light as the weird clutching sensation he'd felt earlier—when she'd been so impressed with his hundred-buck gratuity, and again when she'd looked at him as if he'd given her something precious in Buena Vista Park—returned.

He wasn't gallant—not even close. And he didn't want to be. He took her hand in his and lifted her fingers to his lips. Time to get the night back on track. If she wanted gallant, he knew how to fake it.

'So, are we good to go?' he asked, lifting his eyebrows in a deliberately lascivious way that had her choking out another of those musical giggles.

'I don't think that was ever in doubt,' she said, but then the blush seemed to intensify again. 'But that's not what I wanted to talk to you about. It's to do with my work for Zachary Temple and Temple Corp.' She tugged her fingers from his, stumbling over the words. 'I'm here to—' He touched his finger to her lips to cut her off.

'Shh…' he said. 'It doesn't matter,' he added.

He'd heard of the British billionaire businessman's reputation as a smart investor. Once upon a time Luke would have had to go cap in hand to a guy like him. But not any more. Not since he'd taken his company global and pushed his income and his industry cachet into the stratosphere. Thank the lord.

Perhaps she figured he was planning to prise information out of her about her boss? Or pitch for investment.

He should be insulted. He didn't need investment, or to impress men like Temple any more. And he sure as heck didn't need to mix business with booty calls. Broussard Tech had taken the tech industry by storm because it produced quality, innovative, unique products. Not because he used sex to further his business interests.

But, strangely, he wasn't insulted—he suspected her hesitancy wasn't because she was judging him, but because she was judging herself. He'd never met a woman before who was such a knockout but seemed so unaware of it.

He guessed it was one of the things he found so refreshing about her. But he did not want her nerves getting in the way of their booty call. Especially with the rain lashing against the fuselage as the storm arrived in earnest.

'Are you sure?' she said. 'I don't want to sleep with you under false pretences.'

Oh, for the love of...

'Cassandra,' he said, trying to sound firm,

when the words 'sleep with you' in that prim UK accent had made the heat pounding in his pants hit critical mass. 'There's gonna be nothing false about tonight. As far as I'm concerned we left our professional interests back in San Francisco. Anything that happens tonight is between us and only us. You got that?'

She tugged at her lip again with her teeth, torturing him for one more excruciating moment, but then she nodded. 'Okay…if you're sure.'

'I'm sure.' He grasped her hand and tugged her across the console. 'Now, let's get up to the house before we drown.'

Cassie raced up the slick stone steps cut into the cliff-face behind Luke.

She was soaked through in seconds, but it was a warm, revitalising rain, washing away the guilt and the hesitation and leaving behind a freshness, a newness, and a woman committed to making tonight a memory to savour.

The relief was immense—but not nearly as immense as the tidal wave of excitement which swept over her as Luke's house appeared out of the mist and rain, lit by the same solar-powered flares illuminating the steps up from the dock.

The Pacific Ocean churned below them as the wind picked up its pace and the storm arrived in all its glory. The sleek modern structure of glass and steel, redwood and granite, rose out of the rock face in stacked terraces, blending into the surrounding landscape of dense forest and millennia-old volcanic rock.

Oh... My.

She imagined the structure would be glorious in the daylight, when the waves crashed against the rocks, framing its magnificent view over the ocean, but at night it looked dramatic and daring.

Her heartbeat bumped into her throat, and her breathing turned into staggered pants as they reached an arched doorway. Sheltering her with his body, Luke tapped out a code on a security panel. The rain dripped off his brow and soaked into his shirt to reveal the shadow of chest hair and the bulge of muscle and sinew beneath.

The steel entrance door slid open. He dragged her in behind him and flicked a switch. A series of low lights revealed the cathedral-like drama of the living area—two storeys high and fronted by a wall of glass—at the end of the short redwood entrance hall. Cassie glimpsed sunken sofas surrounding a granite firepit, a state-of-the-art kitchen area and an open staircase leading up to a mezzanine.

Luke Broussard's home made a statement, like the man himself. Both were unique and bold and breathtaking.

The entrance door slid closed, shutting out the roar of the storm, and all she could focus on was the distant rattle of water cascading down glass and the staggered sound of her own breathing. And his.

Luke tugged her round to face him. Her gaze became fixated on the magnificent contours of his torso revealed by the translucent shirt.

'You good?' he asked, as his thumb wiped the water from her lips.

'Yes.' The vicious shudder which racked her body had nothing to do with the clammy feel of her soaked clothing, and everything to do with the fire his touch ignited. 'You have an incredible home,' she added, dislodging his hand, desperate to fill the charged silence.

'Glad you approve,' he said, his wry tone turning the shudder of need into something absolutely terrifying.

What on earth was she doing here? She didn't know the first thing about having epic sex. Or even about having one-night stands. She'd never even made love with anyone before, and certainly not with a man as overwhelming as this man.

Had she set herself up to fail? Spectacularly?

What if she disappointed him? What if she disappointed herself?

Seriously, Cassie, what the heck were you

thinking? You're not a free spirit. Or a sexual adventurer. You're a boring workaholic who doesn't know the first thing about satisfying herself, let alone satisfying a man like Luke Broussard.

'Hey.' Grasping her chin between his thumb and forefinger, he brought her gaze back to his. 'I can see you overthinking again.'

A laugh escaped. 'It's what I do best,' she said.

His hand slid down to capture her neck. He nudged her back against the wooden wall of the entrance hall. She could smell him, heat and arousal and pine soap, above the scent of wood resin and fresh rain. Her hands settled on his waist, absorbing the tension in his abs and sending a shock of longing straight to her sex.

His mouth lowered to hers. She stared at his face, the yearning as intense as the fear now.

'Close your eyes, Cassandra,' he demanded, and she obeyed.

Then his lips were on hers at last. She let out a small sob, welcoming him in instinctively. He cupped her cheeks and angled her head so he could delve deeper.

And as he devoured her, every thought, every feeling blasted out of her head bar one.

I want this. I want him. It doesn't matter if I muck it up.

The liberating thought loosened her tongue to tangle with his. Fire spiked in her sex and at every point where their bodies touched as she gave herself permission to fail, for the first time in her life.

He dragged his sodden jacket off her shoulders and dropped it on the hall floor. Grasping her waist, he lifted her, his mouth leaving hers to growl, 'Wrap your legs around me.'

Again she did as she was told, clinging to his broad shoulders as he marched them both across the living area and up the open staircase.

The rain pounded the glass in undulating waves, like the tsunami of sensation battering her body. Hunger surged as they reached the mezzanine level.

A flash of lightning outside revealed a staggering view of the inlet below them and the storm-tossed forest. The trees bowed and buckled against the wind. The turbulent weather and the magnificent sight of nature reaching its nadir was almost as dramatic as the clatter of her heartbeat.

She usually hated the dark. A silly lay-over from childhood which had always embarrassed her. But the usual anxiety failed to materialise now, as her excitement spiked.

He barged backwards into a room off the landing and shouted. 'Lights on!'

The sudden glare illuminated a stunning if sparsely furnished room, dominated by a view of the ocean and the distant sprinkle of lights along the Oregon shoreline miles away. Then Cassie caught sight of her reflection in the dark glass. She buried her face against his neck to hide her burning blush. With her clothes and hair drenched, she was a total mess.

But the moment of panicked vanity lasted less than a second when he murmured, 'Lower...' and the lights dipped to a shadowy glow.

He put her down, still holding her waist. Her legs wobbled, unsteady, unsure. But then his mouth returned to hers—firm, commanding, uncompromising—telling her in no uncertain terms how much he wanted this. How much he wanted her.

He took control, his hands exploring her curves, and exploiting the dazzle of sensation across her chilled skin. She followed his lead, threading her fingers into his wet hair, loving the feel of his hard body against hers.

Thank goodness someone knew what he was doing.

He broke away and his questing fingers paused. He stared at her, his face shadowed by the soft light but fierce with need, and she felt a residual flicker of panic. Had he already figured out what a fraud she was?

'How the hell do I get you out of this thing?' he asked.

The frustration in his voice had a laugh popping out alongside her relief. 'Here,' she said, and lifted her arm to locate the tab.

But before she could lower the zip he took charge again. 'No, let me. I've been dreaming of peeling you out of this all night.'

She nodded and let go, exhilarated by the sharp concentration on his face as he eased the zip down. He skimmed his fingertips over her shoulders to push the dress's straps off. The flash of hunger and desire that darkened his expression only vindicated her more.

No hesitations, Cassie. No regrets.

The gold *lamé*, heavy with water, dropped down and snagged at her waist, leaving her breasts bare.

'No bra…'

He groaned, the sound deep and feral. She crossed her arms over her nakedness instinctively.

'Don't…' he murmured, the word half-command, half-plea.

Taking her wrists gently in his, he lifted her arms free, his gaze branding her. Her nipples— already pebbled from the cold—squeezed into painful peaks. He swore, and circled his thumb over one, then the other. *'Belle…'*

She shuddered, her emotion as powerful as her desire when his gaze locked on hers. Naked need echoed deep in her sex.

'You cold, *cher*?' he asked, the gruff question making it sound as if he were having trouble speaking English.

She shook her head, speech deserting her completely.

If this is just a one-night stand, why does it feel so intense?

Cradling her heavy breasts, so sensitive now that she couldn't stop shivering, he sent her a lazy smile, but fierce passion filled his eyes.

'Let's warm you up anyhow,' he said.

Then he bent his head and captured one engorged peak between firm lips.

She sobbed, her fingers sinking into his hair to drag him closer, and to keep her knees from buckling as he drew the nipple deep into his mouth. Heat cascaded through her, flooding into her core, the sensation becoming overwhelming as he feasted on the swollen flesh.

He suckled strongly, one breast then the other, until she was weak and aching with need, every point on her body desperate for something more.

At last he released her from the torture and shoved the sodden dress the rest of the way to the floor.

Kneeling, he bent his dark head to touch her

belly. Then he eased off first one sandal, then the other. He skimmed his thumb over the raw spot where the leather had rubbed her heel.

'Ouch,' he said.

But she couldn't feel the pain any more…had stopped noticing it hours ago.

Then he hooked his fingers into her lace panties and eased the damp scrap of material down her legs.

Holding on to his shoulder, she stepped out of her underwear, naked now, while he was still fully clothed.

She'd never felt more exposed, more vulnerable, before in her life. But as he stood up the yearning only pulsed harder in her sex. Her head barely reached his collarbone.

'You're wearing too many clothes,' she managed, folding her arms over her breasts, still damp from his lips.

He nodded, his eyes glassy with desire, then ripped his shirt loose from his trousers, dragged it over his head without unbuttoning it to reveal the sculpted beauty of his naked chest. The strong lines bunched as he moved. The tanned skin was marked by several small scars, and the black ink which ringed his collarbone was not barbed wire, she realised, but a tangle of thorns.

He had other tattoos. One on his bicep of a bird of some kind, and a line of text in French—

or probably French Cajun—arrowing into the dark line of hair which bisected his six-pack. But before she could read the words, or attempt a translation, he kicked off his shoes, unbuckled his belt, ripped open his fly and shoved off his trousers and boxers.

Her mind blurred as his magnificent erection—hard, thick and long—stood proud from the thicket of hair at his groin.

Moisture flooded her sex and dried in her throat. She reached out to run her fingertip down the thick length.

He made a tortured sound and the massive erection jerked against her touch. But then he grabbed her wrist to pull her hand away. 'Don't...'

'I'm so sorry,' she blurted out, meeting his eyes. 'I didn't mean to...'

'Don't apologise,' he said, his tone raw. 'But we'll have to take a rain-check on the foreplay.'

A rain-check? There's going to be a next time?

Something that felt disturbingly like joy burst in her chest, but then he scooped her up and placed her onto the bed. She bounced on the coverlet, the tumultuous feeling only intensifying as the storm continued to rage outside, matching the thunder in her chest.

He knelt over her, trapping her under his big

body as he reached into the bedside table and located a foil packet. He tore it open with his teeth, and she watched him sheath himself with the protection.

She braced herself, ready for him to plunge deep into her yearning sex, but instead he moved down, cradled her hips in strong hands and sank his face between her legs.

He trailed his tongue up her inner thigh, sipping and licking, and she bucked off the bed.

'Ahh…' she cried, the sound as incoherent as her thoughts, her feelings.

He parted her with his thumbs and blew on the molten bundle of nerves already throbbing painfully. Then he swirled his tongue through the slick folds.

'Please…' Her cries became louder, as she begged, so shocked by the pleasure battering her body she could hardly breathe. 'Just…'

'Just what, *cher*?' He looked up, his smile as devastating as the crash of thunder outside. 'You know you taste even better than you smell?'

'I… *Really?*' she asked, then realised how ridiculous she sounded when he gave a deep, husky laugh. But before she could become embarrassed he licked her again—right…*there*.

She shuddered…sobbed. Then he closed his lips over the swollen nub and flicked his tongue across it. She bucked, writhed, desperate to escape the torture, but just as desperate to have it never end. He held her steady, held her open as he worked the tender nub. The wave gathered—strong, fast, too furious to bear.

Everything inside her clenched tight, bearing down. She moaned, her body arching up, bowing back, straining, desperate. Then she flew apart. The orgasm shattered her, cascading through her body like the waves crashing onto the rocks below.

She sank back to the bed, her body floating on a golden tide of afterglow.

His face appeared above her. *'Encore,'* he demanded.

He angled her hips, his erection butting against her sex. And before she had a moment to brace herself he plunged home.

She flinched, the penetration immense, the full, stretched feeling too much.

He stopped, embedded to the hilt as she struggled to adjust.

'So tight, *cher…*' he murmured, the gruff tone tortured. 'You okay?'

She nodded, her sex pulsing around the thick intrusion, the slice of pain thankfully receding.

'You're not a virgin, are you, *cher*?' he asked, and the frown was back, his tone rough with astonishment.

She shook her head vigorously, suddenly desperate not to have him know the truth or this moment would take on a far greater significant than it already had.

He waited, searching her face as he held her hips, and didn't move.

'Really, I'm not…it's just been a while,' she finally managed, hating the lie, but hating the miserable feeling of inadequacy that she remembered far too well from her childhood more.

He nodded, and at last he began to move. But emotion scraped against her throat.

The pleasure ignited again—a flicker, then a throb in the deepest recesses of her body. It built and built as he rocked his hips, finding a rhythm that propelled her with staggering speed back towards that terrifying edge.

She clung to him as she had on the bike, her fingers slipping on his sweat-slicked skin. He grunted, growing huge inside the tight sheath. Her throat closed, and she felt the emotion gathering in her chest to form a fist, punching against her ribs.

The pleasure turned to exquisite pain, hurtling towards her. So fierce, so furious, she couldn't think any more. All she could do was feel… Until the wave rammed into her at last and he made her fly once more.

CHAPTER FOUR

Ash. Help! I slept with Luke last night! Luke Broussard of Broussard Tech. The guy I'm supposed to be checking out for Temple. What do I do now? I'm freaking out. You have to help me. You so owe me, Ms Don't-Wear-a-Bra-with-That-Dress. xx

LUKE PROPPED HIS shoulder against the kitchen doorframe and watched Cassandra furiously tapping with her thumbs and chewing on her bottom lip while she typed what looked like a novel into her cell phone. She kept pausing and looking into the middle distance, then tapping some more. But he could tell by the pucker on her brow that she wasn't seeing the ocean beneath the cove, quiet now, and gilded by a bright new day after last night's storm.

His body tightened. As it had so many times during the night. He eased himself upright, careful not to make a sound. He didn't want to alert her to his presence—not yet—only too aware of the storm in his gut which still hadn't been tamed. And the storm in his chest which refused to go away.

Jesus, how could she look even more stunning, with her tangled, sleep-mussed hair tumbling over her shoulders, her bare legs going on for miles under the T-shirt she must have snagged from his dresser while he was comatose?

Heat bloomed in his gut and he tensed. By rights he should be well satisfied and still comatose. From the angle of the sun, filtering through the forest behind the house on the east side of the inlet, it wasn't much past nine. But when he'd woken up, he'd reached for her and found her gone. And then he'd seen the spots of blood on the bed sheets. And he had wondered, just as he had suspected when he'd thrust heavily inside her last night and felt her flinch... Had she been a virgin after all?

And, if so, why had she lied?

Waking up with an erection was nothing new. But why did the possibility of her virginity make it seem more intense? She might be inexperienced, but she was a grown woman. How the hell she might have managed to stay untouched for so long, he had no idea, but it was her choice—he hadn't pushed or pressured her—in fact he'd gone out of his way to do the opposite. She'd even accused him of being 'gallant' for the first time in his entire life.

He hadn't exploited her or taken anything from her she hadn't been willing to give.

And if she *had* been a virgin, it didn't make him a bad guy.

But, as he continued to watch her unobserved, something told him that for the first time in his life, with Cassandra James, all the usual rules didn't apply. She'd changed them. And he didn't like it. Because normally after a one-night booty call he'd be looking to find a way to get her out of his home without things getting too awkward. But instead all he could think about right now was walking up behind her, wrapping his arms around her waist, inhaling that glorious scent which had invaded his dreams last night and finding out if she'd picked him to be her first lover. And if she had, why had she?

But how could he do that without making this even more intense and awkward? Even more weird? Why had he broken his own rules with her, bringing her here?

Would she expect something from him now? Something more than pleasure? Even though he hoped he'd made it clear he couldn't offer her more?

He felt a strange contraction in his chest as

he imagined her turning round and opening her arms to him with the same enthusiasm and spontaneity she'd shown last night.

He frowned.

How did she do that? How did she make him forget that this situation was now all kinds of screwed up? He couldn't touch her again. It would only make him feel more invested.

Whatever happened now, he needed to lay off her until he could get her off the island.

Perhaps she was expecting him to ask again about her virginity—but he wasn't falling into that trap.

Why did it have to be a big deal? They were both adults. And the sex had been incredible. She'd been so responsive, so cute and sweet and hot and uninhibited. No reason to make this anything else than what it had always been intended to be. And if she brought it up—which she probably would eventually, because why else would she have kept her virginity a secret other than to use it at a later date—he'd tell her the truth: that her virginity was her business and had nothing to do with him.

She finally stopped tapping on her phone and placed it on the countertop. The sharp click of metal against granite echoed in the silent room. But she continued to stare at her phone as if it might leap up and bite her. Kind of the way she'd stared at the bike helmet the night before, until she'd decided to take it.

He cleared his throat, deciding it was time to stop thinking and start doing. He needed to get past the awkwardness so he could get her off his island.

She spun round. A blush blazed across her cheeks and hunger fired through his gut on cue.

He forced a smile to his lips. *Relax, man.* 'Good morning, *cher*,' he said.

Her gaze dipped to his naked chest, then shot back up again as the blush climbed to her hairline. After everything they'd done last night, he wouldn't have thought it was physically possible for her to continue to blush so readily. Unfortunately, it only confirmed what he already knew. Virgin or not, she had not been as experienced as she'd made out.

He crossed the kitchen, then sank his hands into the pockets of his sweats in order to resist the powerful urge to cradle her cheeks and feel the heat from her skin seep into his palms.

You're not gonna jump her again. Remember?

'How you doing?' he asked, because she looked hesitant—in a way she hadn't been last night.

'I'm…great, thank you,' she said, her bright tone brittle.

He let it slide and fisted his fingers in his

pants' pockets to resist the powerful urge to touch.

'The storm has passed,' she said, turning to study the view as if her life depended on it.

'Yeah,' he said, studying her instead. So they were going to talk about the weather. 'Not too much damage done.'

'Do they usually?' she asked, her eyes widening as she turned back towards him. 'Cause damage? The storms? It was so overwhelming last night. I wouldn't be at all surprised.'

He wondered if they were really talking about the weather, or something else entirely, as her blush continued to glow.

'I'll need to do a thorough check before I know for sure,' he said.

The splash of colour on her cheeks went scarlet.

Nope, not talking about the weather at all.

He braced himself, waiting for her to address the huge elephant in the room.

But all she said was, 'I see.'

Her gaze skimmed over his bare chest again, and the heat in his gut blossomed. He tensed, but then his stomach rumbled loud enough to be heard in Washington State.

At least this was one hunger he could satisfy.

'You want some breakfast? I could make pancakes?' he said, then frowned.

When was the last time he had offered to cook a woman breakfast? Probably never. Especially when he was supposed to be trying to get rid of her.

'That would be wonderful, but I really don't want to put you to too much trouble before we fly back to the city.'

The casual mention of their trip back surprised him. Truth was, it should have relieved him. If she wasn't going to make a big deal about last night that was good, right? But it didn't relieve him. Somehow it just annoyed him more. She'd dropped a bombshell into their casual one-night booty call and now she thought she could just ignore it? Seriously?

'No trouble,' he said. 'Why don't you grab the eggs and milk out of the fridge?' he added, needing to keep things short and sweet.

He'd cook her pancakes and then take her back to the city. End of. That was what they'd arranged.

She returned with the fixings and he set about making the batter.

'Do you need me to do anything?' she asked.

'No, I've got this,' he said, cracking the eggs into the bowl one-handed and trying not to notice the way his old T-shirt inched up her thighs when she perched on one of the stools at the breakfast bar.

The sudden blast of heat as he recalled having those long, supple limbs hooked around his waist had him scattering the flour a bit too generously as he added it to the mixture.

'You're very good at that,' she said.

'Yeah,' he murmured, still distracted by the smooth, toned skin as she crossed her legs. 'I was a short-order cook in a diner the whole of my sophomore year in high school,' he added, to distract himself from the heat starting to pound again in his pants.

'Was that one of those minimum wage jobs you were talking about yesterday?' she asked. 'In the small town near Lafayette?'

'Sure, but this was *in* Lafayette. Nobody would hire me in my hometown,' he said, trying not to get fixated on the memory of how sweet she'd tasted when he'd…

'Why not?' she asked, sounding upset, and the indignant tone interrupted his wayward thoughts.

'Because of my old man's reputation.' He picked up the whisk and dragged his gaze away from the danger zone.

You're not jumping her again, Broussard, this booty call is over.

'That seems very unfair.'

'Huh?' he said, having totally lost the thread of their conversation.

'Why should you be blamed for your father's bad reputation?'

He stared at her sympathetic expression as the guileless question registered and the slow throb of his pulse became a gallop.

Hang on a minute? He'd told her *that*? What the…?

He *never* spoke about his father, or that time in his life. Certainly not to a hook-up. Because he'd gone to some pains to cover it up when he'd been starting out. He hadn't wanted his father's crimes tarnishing his company the way they had tarnished so much of his childhood and adolescence. But now, as she stared at him, the concern in her gaze had his ribs feeling tight. The way they had during the night, when he'd held her in his arms as they'd both dropped into sleep.

His galloping pulse charged into his throat.

Hell, no. They were not going to have this conversation. Talking about his old man was off-limits.

'How about you go find yourself something to wear in the housekeeper's annexe while I get these done? Mrs Mendoza's about your size— you can get to it through the mud room.'

He had to get her out of that thigh-skimming T and into something a lot more substantial before he got so damn distracted he ended up blurting out his whole life story.

'I'm guessing the gold dress is a write-off,' he added.

'Um…yes—yes, it is.'

Her eyes widened, and a flush rose up her throat—making him almost feel bad for changing the subject so abruptly. *Almost.*

'Won't Mrs Mendoza think it's a bit odd that I came all this way with no clothes,' she asked, as the blush hit her cheeks.

And then he figured out the cause of her embarrassment. This had to be the first time in her life she'd ever done the walk of shame after a booty call.

His ribs contracted again. *Bingo, buddy! Now you feel even more invested. Terrific.*

'Mrs Mendoza's not here,' he said, his tone gruffer and more impatient than he had intended. 'I get the staff to vacate when I'm on the island,' he added. 'Like I said, I prefer my privacy. Take whatever you need and I'll make sure she's reimbursed.'

'Oh, okay…'

Her gaze flickered away from his face and he felt like a jerk, which didn't improve his mood at all.

She slipped off the stool, and her unfettered breasts bounced enticingly under the soft cotton of his old T. A shaft of heat hit him square in the gut. It came with a brutal side order of regret that he wouldn't be able to feast on those ripe, responsive nipples again.

'I'll go and see what I can find,' she said, flicking a thumb over her shoulder. 'And be back ASAP.'

'Don't rush on my account,' he said, going the full jerk and trying not to care. Better she knew this was the end of the road. 'The batter needs to sit for a while before I start flipping.'

She'd complicated things with her possible virginity. Made him feel responsible in a way he never had before and blurt out stuff he'd never told anyone. Not to mention deal with the worst case of FOMO known to man as his gaze tracked the sweet, sultry sway of her hips under the butt-skimming T-shirt as she headed for the mud room.

The journey back to the city in his seaplane, surrounded by her scent and tortured by memories of last night, was going to be an hour-long lesson in sexual frustration.

He'd just sprinkled some more flour into the egg and milk mixture, trying to concentrate on getting through the next couple of hours without losing what was left of his mind, when he heard a rattling hum and spotted Cassandra's cell phone, vibrating against the granite countertop. He picked it up, intending to switch it off, but caught sight of the notification that flashed onto the home screen.

His brows drew down as he read the message from someone identified as 'Ash'.

His stomach twisted into a painful knot and suddenly sexual frustration was the least of his worries, as the cruel wave of betrayal washed through him like acid.

CHAPTER FIVE

'Would you like a hand with the pancakes?' Cassie asked, trying to sound calm and casual and totally cool.

Not easy when she felt anything but.

Especially after Luke had caught her earlier in nothing but his T-shirt and her knickers. He'd been tense and guarded and *off*, somehow, and what had been exciting and freeing last night—a sexual adventure to be proud of—now just made her feel exposed… And unbelievably awkward.

Still, at least she had some clothes on now. Even if they did belong to someone else. She had drawn the line at borrowing his housekeeper's underwear, but she'd managed to find a pair of jeans and a baggy T-shirt and sweater and some boots and socks.

She'd left a thank-you note on the housekeeper's kitchen table in the annexe, with a promise to have the clothes returned once she'd had them cleaned.

With her hair tied in a knot after she'd taken a quick shower in one of the guest bathrooms, she still felt hopelessly exposed, though. She didn't have on any of her usual armour. She didn't even have her make-up with her... Or a bra!

Gee, thanks, Ash.

Luke sat on a kitchen stool, his head bent over something. He hadn't heard her offer to help—probably a good thing, she decided, seeing as she knew next to nothing about making pancakes.

She took a moment to absorb the sight of him. A sight that still had the power to stagger her.

Her breathing became ragged. Again.

She still couldn't quite believe everything that had happened...or how immense it had seemed. That a man who looked like he did, who oozed heat and passion and sex appeal from every pore, hadn't just noticed her, but had seduced her so thoroughly, with such power and passion and such dedication to her pleasure as well as his own.

One thing was certain. However grumpy he might be in the mornings, Luke Broussard came into his own at night.

A small smile tilted her lips, but then wavered and flattened as she caught her reflection in the window glass and the awkwardness returned.

Unfortunately, while she looked less than her

best, Luke Broussard, even in nothing more than a pair of sweatpants, looked drop-dead gorgeous. The smooth tanned skin on his bare chest and broad shoulders gleamed in the sunshine coming through the floor-to-ceiling windows, highlighting the tattoo of thorns that ringed his collarbone.

The thousand and one thoughts that had been bombarding her ever since she'd woken up that morning, to find him fast asleep beside her, her body aching and her mind a mass of confusion, began to batter her all over again.

Not one of those thoughts, though, was calm or cool or casual.

All the problems with what she'd done—what *they'd* done—had only increased her confusion and anxiety in the past twenty minutes, while she'd taken a shower and tried to get a handle on how to deal with the awkwardness of her first ever morning-after…

She had no doubt last night had been about chemistry and fun for Luke, but she could see now that it had been about more than that for her. And that was without even factoring in the lie she'd told him about her virginity.

She'd tried to tell herself it wasn't a big deal. But when he'd treated her so dismissively this morning it had hurt when it really shouldn't have. Why hadn't she thought this through?

Being stuck on an island with the guy you'd had your first ever sexual encounter with was bound to be awkward. Practicalities-wise, it was a nightmare. Not only had she been forced to borrow his housekeeper's clothes, she couldn't leave under her own steam. She was completely reliant on him flying her out of here.

She coughed, trying to clear the swell of anxiety from her throat.

Luke's head lifted sharply.

What she saw on his face had her drawing in a sharp breath. This was more than impatience. Much more. His jaw was rigid with tension as he stared at her, his gaze flat and hard...

'You're back,' he said.

His voice was as harsh and flat as his gaze, the husky purr which had intoxicated her all through the night gone.

'You've got some explaining to do.'

The accusing words came out like brittle staccato punches, confusing her more. Until he lifted the hand he had on the counter and she spotted her smartphone.

'Tell me, did Temple tell you to screw me while you were spying on me? Or was I just lucky?'

'I...? What?' she choked, shocked by the barely leashed fury in his tone—and the crude accusation. 'I wasn't spying on you...'

'Cut the BS. I've got evidence.'

He got off the stool and stalked towards her, the fury on his face becoming thunderous. Snagging her wrist, he slapped her phone into her palm.

'Read it,' he sneered, the command in his voice low with disdain. 'Then explain yourself.'

She clicked on the touch screen to find a notification of Ash's reply to her earlier text...

You slept with the fella Temple sent you to spy on??? OMG! The dress was even more deadly than I thought.

Cassie stiffened. And wanted to die on the spot.

A thousand and one ways she could defend herself against Luke Broussard's claims flashed past. She'd never asked him for any information about his business. She'd tried to tell him why she had originally been sent to San Francisco by her boss and he'd shut her down.

But the fury and disgust on his face and the rigid stance of his body made all the denials freeze on her tongue. Because they reminded her of all the times she had tried to defend herself against the disapproval of another man. Suddenly she was a little girl again, bullied and belittled by her father and always, *always* found wanting.

'No wonder you were so damn interested in my old man's reputation,' he sneered. 'All part of the background check for your boss.'

She curled her fingers around the phone and shook her head. 'I wasn't asking for Temple. I just… It seemed so unfair. And I—'

'Yeah, right…' He cut her off again. 'And to think I thought you were a virgin there for a minute.'

Cassie recoiled at the bitterness in his accusation. How had he guessed the truth?

'That's one hell of an act you've got going,' he added.

She stepped back, away from the fury emanating off him. She knew he wouldn't hurt her—not physically…that wasn't the kind of man he was—but she could see he was only holding on to his temper with an effort. And she couldn't engage with it. Because it would make her feel small and insignificant and defenceless, the way she had felt so many times as a child.

'I didn't come here to spy on you,' she said again, her hands shaking now. How ironic that she hadn't wanted him to know about her inexperience, and somehow he'd found a way to use it against her anyway. 'I should go,' she said.

'Ya think?' he sneered.

She needed to get away, humiliated now by the heat and longing still rippling through her body. How could she still respond to him when he had changed from the man she'd thought she knew to someone cruel and suspicious and judgemental?

But before she'd gone five steps his voice tore through her.

'Just so you know,' he added, 'when we get back to the city I'm gonna be talking to my lawyers.'

She swung round. What was he saying?

'I… I don't understand,' she said, keeping her voice even while her insides were turning into a gelatinous mass. How could she have put her career, and everything she'd worked for into so much jeopardy?

'You snuck in here to get insider dope on me and my business for your boss. No way am I letting you use what you learned against me.'

The brutal pressure in her chest increased as the heat of his fury emanated off his skin, making his biceps bulge as he planted his hands in the pockets of his sweatpants. Unfortunately, that shifted the waistband of his pants lower, revealing the line of his hip flexors and the text of his tattoo—which read *Laissez les bon temps rouler*, she had discovered that morning, when she'd woken up in a sleepy haze and found him lying next to her.

Heat pulsed and glowed at her core. Damning her even more.

'But I didn't find out anything compromising about you,' she blurted out, ignoring the painful tightening in her chest. 'And even if I did, I would never use it against you. Not after—'

'How dumb do you think I am?'

She heard it then—the insecurity beneath the anger—and suddenly she knew that the high school boy who had been ostracised in his hometown because of something his father had done still lurked inside this man, defensive and guarded. She couldn't talk to this man, couldn't make any of this right. The only thing to do now was to leave and hope she could repair what was left of her career and her self-respect. She'd fallen into his arms far too easily, given him something of herself she had never intended to give, and ended up being punished for it.

'I'll meet you at the plane,' she said, feeling stupidly raw because she had given him so much ammunition… And for what? For a passing moment of physical pleasure…the chance to throw caution to the wind for the first time in her life. It had been exhilarating and exciting, and so much more than she had ever expected. But now she would be forced to pay the price for her naivete and her stupidity. 'I think it's probably best we leave as soon as possible.'

His biceps flexed, making him even more imposing. Dark brows lowered over those blazing green eyes, drawing her gaze to the small scar she'd wondered about several times during the night. But then the hard line of his jaw tightened.

'At least that's one damn thing we can agree on,' he said.

Turning away from her, he stalked back to the kitchen island, the rigid line of his shoulders suggesting he wasn't as calm and collected as he was trying to make out.

Unfortunately, that wasn't much comfort for the pain digging its claws into her belly as she headed across the kitchen on unsteady legs towards the stairs.

The last of her once glorious adventure had disintegrated, the hideous reality of it revealed, as humiliation and anxiety tangled in her gut.

And one miserable thought reverberated in her head.

How on earth am I going to survive an hour in a tiny plane with him when he hates my guts?

'We can't leave.'

Thirty minutes later Cassie stood on the dock

with her evening purse and the torn gold dress stuffed into a backpack she'd borrowed from the housekeeper's annexe. Her whole body was shaking as she tried to absorb what Luke had just barked at her.

'What do you mean, we can't leave?' she said, trying to keep the tremble of panic out of her voice.

Surely she could not have heard him correctly? He wanted her gone as much as she wanted to be gone. She needed to be gone, like, yesterday if she was going to have any chance whatsoever of preserving the remnants of her tattered dignity until this dreadful day was over.

'The plane's damaged. The Wi-Fi went down last night and the cell phone service went out twenty minutes ago, while I was talking to the mechanic,' he said, his face implacable.

'But…'

But I can't stay on Sunrise—not with you… not now. Not after the things you accused me of.

'Don't you have a boat?' she asked, becoming more frantic by the second.

Her phone had lost its service too, but she had actually been grateful for it, having no idea what she was supposed to say to Ash now.

Ash's jokey text had landed her in trouble with Luke, but she knew Ash wasn't the one to blame for her predicament. Not even close.

Eventually Luke would have found out the truth about Temple's interest in his company and assumed the worst.

Their one wild night had been brought about by pheromones and insanity—on her part, at least—and she hadn't stopped to think about how it would all play out because she hadn't really cared at the time. Luke Broussard had unleashed feelings she had never known she was even capable of, and she'd ridden that adrenaline rush to its inevitable car crash conclusion.

She could see that clearly now. She should never have taken the risks she had with a man she barely knew. A man who clearly had serious trust issues she knew nothing about. But she had at least hoped she might be able to mitigate the worst of the fallout from this disaster when she got back to San Francisco.

She had come up with a course of action while raiding Mrs Mendoza's living quarters a second time. She would simply tell Temple the truth—or as much of the truth as was required. That she had lost her objectivity with Luke Broussard, but that she knew he wasn't interested in attracting investors.

Temple had in no way been committed to investing in Broussard Tech…this had simply been a fact-finding mission. She still had time to come up with other investment opportunities in the Bay Area, using the contacts he'd given her.

She had planned to use the flight back to the city to soothe Luke Broussard's temper and get him to call off his plans to sue. She knew how to handle difficult billionaires after three years working for Temple—although she had to admit Temple was considerably less volatile than Luke. But she'd never been drawn to her boss the way she'd so stupidly been drawn to this man. Surely she could use that, somehow, to make Luke see he was being unreasonable? That following through on his knee-jerk reaction after seeing Ash's inflammatory text would be expensive and unnecessary if Temple dropped any interest in his company?

But all her plans would come to nothing if she was stuck on Sunrise Island for any length of time, without being able to contact her boss or do the job he'd sent her to San Francisco to do.

Not only that, she didn't think she could hold herself together if she had to spend any more time alone with Luke Broussard.

A surge of distress at the prospect made her heartbeat ricochet into her throat.

'Yeah, I have a speedboat,' he said, grinding out the answer as if she had no right to even ask. 'But the power's out by the boathouse, which means I'm gonna have to hand-crank the doors to get it out, and I don't like the look of the weather.'

He thrust his fingers through his hair, then glanced up at the sky just as a dark cloud crossed over the sun.

'It's an hour's ride to the mainland from here,' he added. 'And I'm not risking the journey just to please you when another storm could drop any minute.'

'Right…' she said, feeling her own jaw tightening. Really? Did he have to be quite so much of a pill? Hadn't he given her enough grief already? 'So are you saying we might be stuck here for another hour or two?'

His flat gaze met hers. 'We're stuck here until I say it's safe to leave.' Each word was drawn out to make it abundantly clear he was the one in charge. 'Which could be days, not hours.'

'You can't be serious…' she murmured, shock reverberating through her body.

Days? Dear God.

'Don't get your panties in a twist. This is a hell of a lot worse for me than it is for you,' he said, disgust dripping from every word.

'How can it be worse for you?' she began. 'You're not the one who has been accused of—'

'Stop bugging me and go back to the house and wait,' he said, slicing her distressed defence right down to the bone, the way he had done earlier. Without giving her a chance to explain.

Bugging him? How dare he?

Her temper sparked and sizzled as she opened her mouth to snap back at him. But when his eyes flared, the challenge in them unmistakable, she swallowed down the retort.

He *wanted* her to argue with him. So he could feel superior and vindicated and display more of his temper. She refused to give him the satisfaction.

As a child she'd always backed down in the face of her father's disdain, and it had left her feeling hollow and inadequate. But now, as she forced herself to nod and swung round to make her way back to the house, she didn't feel cowed—she felt righteous. Confronting him about his snotty attitude was not going to help her cause.

Unfortunately, though, the moment of righteousness didn't last long as the truth of their situation began to sink in as she climbed the stairs from the dock. Panic and anxiety turned into a brick in the pit of her stomach as she reached the porch and stared out across her island prison.

The view across the inlet had distress churning under her breastbone.

Last night's storm was visible in the bent and broken branches of the lush evergreens which grew from the rocky crags that formed the cove. A rainbow shimmered over the headland as the bright morning sun hit the mist clinging to the shoreline.

Her throat thickened. The staggering beauty of Luke Broussard's home drew forth memories from the night before which had been haunting her ever since she woke up.

Luke's hands on her, his lips, his mouth, touching, tracing, tempting, tormenting... Helping her to discover pleasures she'd never even known her body was capable of.

But it wasn't just the sex that had seduced her, she thought miserably. It was the way he'd held her afterwards, stroking her hair, murmuring nonsense into the darkness...

Nonsense he probably said to every woman he slept with.

She blinked and blocked out the staggering beauty of the landscape, attempting to block out the memories still torturing her, too—memories that were all false. She'd imbued last night with a significance it had never had. It had been about sex and only sex. Nothing more than a cataclysmic physical connection which had blindsided her because she had no experience whatsoever of physical intimacy.

She'd been much more vulnerable than she'd realised last night—which had to explain all the foolish, reckless, wrong decisions she'd made. Decisions which, ultimately, she had to own.

Yes, Luke was behaving like a domineering, bad-tempered jerk, but she needed to suck up her disdain and make the best of it. And hope like hell he could find a way off the island quickly… Because spending another night here with him was not something she wanted to contemplate, let alone actually negotiate.

At least with him busy she would have a little respite from that judgemental glare—and supersnotty attitude.

Her stomach grumbled as she dumped her borrowed backpack in the entrance hall. She pressed her hand to it. Her rising irritation was not sitting very well with her hunger and her anxiety. First things first: she needed to eat.

Opening the fridge, she spotted the pancake batter he'd made earlier but never had the chance to use. She blinked away the sting in her eyes, stupidly reminded of his offer to make her breakfast—before he'd spotted Ashling's text and turned into Cro-Magnon man.

Ignoring the sealed container, she reached for some cold cuts. She'd never been very good in the domestic sphere. She'd never had to learn more than the absolute basics when it came to home catering—cereal and takeaway—so making pancakes was out. Which was a good thing.

Because having a congenial breakfast with the man was also not going to happen now.

She poured herself a cup of the lukewarm coffee dregs sitting at the bottom of the state-of-the-art coffee maker on the counter. *Terrific.* She was probably going to need an engineering degree from NASA to figure out how to use that, too.

After hunting down some sliced rye bread, she began slapping pieces down on the countertop with a lot more force than was strictly necessary, while indulging in a stress-busting fantasy of slapping the bread against Luke Broussard's granite-hard skull.

But then an idea occurred to her. And she seized on it for no other reason than it allowed her to feel a little more in control… A little more herself again after twenty-four hours of losing herself and becoming someone she didn't even recognise—that crazy lady who had decided to take a motorbike ride and then a plane journey with a guy who fired her senses but had the manners of a Neanderthal.

The only way to take back control of this disaster was to be the bigger, better person. She was not going to rise to Luke Broussard's outrageous accusations, or lower herself to the level of having a temper tantrum over something that could not be changed.

And, to prove it, she would have a magnificent sandwich waiting for him when he came in. Because they would both need to eat before they could take a boat to the mainland…and never see each other again.

The charm offensive she'd planned for the plane journey was not a good idea until they actually got on their way, because it was going to be a titanic effort to maintain it while he was being so difficult. And, knowing him, he'd probably misconstrue her motives and think she was using her nefarious seduction skills to prise precious information about his company out of him.

The jerk.

She scoffed loudly, knowing that no one could hear her. For goodness' sake—if he only knew how ridiculous that scenario was. How the heck could she be Mata Hari when she had so little experience of sex and no experience of seduction whatsoever? But she'd be damned if she'd defend herself against those ludicrous accusations.

And the truth was, on careful consideration, she would much rather he cast her in the role of scheming *femme fatale* than simpering virgin. How much more compromised would she feel right now if he knew she had chosen him to be her first lover? Or how much those moments had meant to her?

The guy already had an ego the size of Oregon.

She slapped slices of baloney and cheese onto the bread, then slathered the sandwiches in mayonnaise and mustard, even more determined to take the moral high ground and extend this olive branch to him—thus treating his snotty attitude with the contempt it deserved…even if it killed her.

Swallowing her temper now, in a way he had been unable to swallow his, wouldn't just make her the better person, it would show him he hadn't rattled her or upset her—far from it… Unlike her father, he didn't have the power to hurt her. All he had the power to do was infuriate her. And if she didn't show him how infuriated she was, he wouldn't even have the satisfaction of doing that.

Ultimately, by rising above his sulky behaviour she could take a huge chunk out of his superiority complex. And on a professional level her strategy was a win-win, too. Because saving her job mattered. Stopping him from suing her or Temple Corp mattered. What had happened last night and what he thought of her did not.

She finished making his sandwich, then left it with a curt note on the countertop before taking her own sandwich to eat in one of the guest bedrooms.

She would learn from this experience, and next time she got offered a ride on a seaplane to a private island for one wild night of pleasure, by a volatile, super-hot, brooding billionaire with a chip on his shoulder the size of a redwood, she would run full-tilt in the opposite direction.

Her stomach continued to churn, though, as she forced herself to consume every bite—while the brick in her belly resolutely refused to go away.

Please, please, don't let me be stuck here for another night.

CHAPTER SIX

LUKE TRUDGED UP the stairs carved into the rock wall that led from the dock as sunset burst over the horizon. He barely spared a glance for the spectacular light show of reds and oranges bleeding into the cerulean blue of the sky, so dog-tired he was ready to face-plant on every agonising step.

And more frustrated than he had ever been in his life.

No way was he getting his overnight guest off the island any time soon.

He'd managed to crank open the doors to the boathouse, only to discover the boat's hull had been damaged in last night's storm too. Not only that, but when his cell service had come back for a half-hour he'd checked the local shipping forecast and seen a number of weather warnings that made any attempt to make it to the mainland in the next couple of days—even if he fixed the boat—not a good idea.

Exhaustion dragged at his heels and made his shoulders sag.

Jezebel was a write-off too, until he could get a plane mechanic out here—and that wasn't happening for the next few days either, because of the weather forecast.

After confronting that reality he'd kayaked to Pirates' Cove on the opposite end of the island and taken his daily swim, trying to calm himself down enough to function again. Even in summer the water had been satisfyingly freezing. Then, to keep his mind off the woman now camped out in his house—and his head—he'd spent the rest of the day circumnavigating the island's ten miles of shoreline to check for any more damage.

His home was the only major structure on Sunrise, and it had survived unscathed, and he'd repaired some broken shingles on the boathouse roof before heading home to give himself time to think.

As much as he wanted Cassandra gone, the fact that he couldn't get her off the island in the next few days meant he had a couple of options. He could take time out from his hard-earned vacation time to repair the boat's hull himself…or he could do what he'd originally intended to do before he'd met Cassandra James—spend the week getting some much-needed downtime on his private island, and she would just have to stay the hell out of his way.

His eyes stung as he brushed sea-matted hair off his forehead, and heat pulsed beneath his wetsuit on cue. He drew in a harsh breath and shoved open the door to the mud room. *Damn it*. Even though he was exhausted, she still had the power to make him ache.

A vision of her as she had looked ten hours ago in his kitchen—wearing his oversized T-shirt, her hair tied on top of her head in a haphazard knot—blasted back into his brain and he tensed.

She hadn't even tried to defend herself. Hadn't even had the decency to admit what she'd done and apologise. If anything, she'd doubled down on her scheme—which was exactly why he wasn't going to let her screw over his vacation. She'd already screwed *him* over enough.

He could control his desire if he put his mind to it.

He needed this break before the product launch.

He and his team had been working on the prototypes for two years, and he hadn't taken any vacation time in almost as long.

Indignation seared his throat as he sat down on the bench and tugged off his board shoes, heat still pulsing defiantly in his lap. And the

memories he'd managed to keep at bay throughout most of the day, through sheer force of will
and hard physical activity, cascaded through
his tired body.

Cassandra draped over his bed, her erect nipples begging for his attention, her eyes dazed
with passion, her body flushed with need, her
scent intoxicating him as he thrust heavily inside her.

He shivered violently. But it wasn't from the
cold, clammy neoprene as he peeled it off.

*Jeez, Broussard, forget about last night, al-
ready. She's the enemy now.*

Everything had been fake: the sweet, sultry
smile, the forthright expression, the live-wire
response which had so intoxicated him, the em-
pathy when he'd let that nugget of information
about his past slip, even the possible evidence of
her virginity. She'd been playing him the whole
time to get what she wanted for her boss.

The heat pulsed harder and he frowned.

Okay, maybe not *everything* had been fake.
No one could fake a response like that. She'd
been as turned on as he was, the memory of her
sex gripping his as she came so vivid it made
the ache in his crotch painful.

Maybe some guys couldn't tell when a woman
was faking an orgasm, but he could tell Cassandra hadn't been faking *that*.

But she'd still played him. And he'd let her.

He picked up the wetsuit and dumped it into the rinsing sink with a loud splat.

Get over it.

It wasn't as if he'd been emotionally invested in their booty call. All he'd wanted out of their night together was great sex, and they'd both got that. So why was his stomach still jumpy and his throat still raw at the thought of her this morning, her chin thrust out, tendrils of wet hair framing her high cheekbones and her translucent skin still reddened from his kisses? Her toned thighs had been rigid with indignation while she'd stared him down and refused to admit how far out of line she was...

Why should he care if she didn't have the decency to come clean and beg for his forgiveness? Business could be dirty. He'd done some things himself he wasn't proud of in the past, to push Broussard Tech to the place it was now.

Temple was obviously a wolf. He got that. He could be ruthless too, when his business was at stake. But to use an employee to seduce him...

Unless...

Was she Temple's lover?

His stomach twisted into a knot at the unbidden thought and something dark and violent rushed through him.

He strode naked into the mud room's power

shower and flicked on the jets. But then the memory of how tight she'd been when he'd entered her that first time came echoing back. And the shock and awe on her face when she'd climaxed. She'd looked overwhelmed.

He didn't trust her, but she'd have to be an award-winning actress to fake *that* response.

His shoulders relaxed a little.

The hot, needle-sharp spray pummelled his cold skin, but as he scrubbed away the salt and sweat of the day's activities the strident erection refused to subside.

Pressing his forehead against the glass bricks, he took himself in hand, jerking his stiff flesh in fast, efficient strokes. Trying to keep Cassandra out of his head, though, proved impossible, the memory of her body caressing his length still vivid as the seed exploded in his hand.

He washed away the evidence, feeling like he had as a teenager after those nights making out under the bleachers—used and dirty.

Not the same thing at all, he told himself. At least those experiences had made him wise to women like Cassandra James ever since. Those girls had shown him that no one could be trusted…that sex was a bargaining chip, just like everything else. He'd finally figured out he didn't need their approval or their affection. And he didn't need Cassandra's.

Nor did he need her to admit what she'd done. All he needed to do was make sure she didn't do his company any damage. Keeping her here for the next few days, maybe even the whole week, didn't necessarily have to be a bad thing. At least if she was stuck on Sunrise, with no cell service, it would save him the trouble of having to brief his legal team to get her to sign an NDA.

He dried himself off and dressed in the sweats he kept in the mud room.

With the edge taken off his need, and the shower having revived him, it occurred to him that he was ravenous. All he'd had since breakfast was a couple of energy bars and a flask of coffee.

He headed into the kitchen.

He had staff for the house—as well as Mrs Mendoza the housekeeper he also employed a maintenance woman and a forester—but, as he'd told Cassandra, he always had them vacate when he was on the island. He hadn't lied when he'd told her he preferred his privacy.

He huffed out a tortured breath.

The irony would almost be funny if it weren't so damn aggravating.

The truth was, the main reason he'd bought Sunrise and built the house was so he could be alone here. He liked his solitude. The outdoor activities available when he needed downtime were a great way to stretch his body as well as his mind. And when he was working on a particularly tough or troublesome new design this was the perfect place to hole up and get it done without any distractions.

Right about now, though, he wished Mrs Mendoza and the rest of his staff were in residence, because he could use a cooked meal without having to do it himself. And having a buffer between him and his resident spy would also be useful.

The sunset cast a reddening glow over the kitchen's granite surfaces, highlighting a mound of something on the main countertop, draped in a paper napkin. He lifted the napkin to find a mountain of bread and cheese and baloney, drenched in enough condiments to sink a battleship.

What the...?

His hollow stomach growled, but not with any particular enthusiasm. Then he noticed the passive-aggressive note jotted down on the napkin.

I made you a sandwich.
You can thank me later.

This mess was supposed to be a sandwich? It looked barely edible. Not only that, but it had clearly been sitting on the counter for the last eight hours. He pressed his finger into the bread to test it… Yup, hard as a slab of concrete.

Wrapping the whole mess in the napkin, he dumped it in the trash can.

He might be starving, but he had standards. And if she thought that pathetic attempt at a peace offering was going to go any way towards appeasing him after what she'd done, she was living on another planet.

By rights she should have taken the damn initiative and cooked them something decent for supper. The house was fully stocked, and she'd been sitting on her butt all day, doing nothing, while he'd been out trying to work out a way to get them off the island. Maybe that wasn't going to happen any time soon, but he'd be damned if he'd let her freeload for the rest of her stay.

If he was going to be forced to keep her here—to keep his company safe from her shenanigans while he took a well-earned break— she could damn well make herself useful.

'Cassandra!' he shouted up the stairs. 'Get down here now. You're on kitchen duty tonight.'

'But I already made you a sandwich.'

Cassie stared at Luke Broussard's hard, handsome face and cursed the flush spreading across her collarbone. She'd figured out several hours ago that they wouldn't be leaving the island tonight. So she'd spent the time trying not to let her anxiety go into free fall while she'd scoped out a bedroom for the night and hunted up a nightlight.

She had raided Mrs Mendoza's closet again for more clothing, just in case Luke's threat of being stuck here for more than one night played out. She did not plan to be unprepared for whatever he might throw at her. She'd also taken the opportunity to do some snooping.

To her astonishment, while looking through the wardrobes in his four guest bedrooms, she hadn't managed to find any leftover clothes from previous girlfriends. Perhaps Luke had actually been telling the truth when he'd told her he'd never brought a woman to the island before... Not that it meant anything. The women he hadn't brought here were the lucky ones—at least they hadn't ended up stranded here.

Satisfied with her haul from Mrs Mendoza's wardrobe, she'd headed to Luke's study in a futile attempt to find an internet connected computer, or at the very least a phone charger in case the coverage returned, because her phone had now died. Unfortunately, the only chargers she'd found were for Broussard Tech phones, and all the computers had elaborate security systems so she hadn't even been able to turn them on, let alone access the internet.

Seriously…who did that? Who had several layers of security on their computers when they were in a study in a locked house on a private island that no one could get to without a plane or a speedboat? Paranoid much?

After nearly an hour spent trying to crack his security, Cassie had returned to the guest room and dropped into a deep, exhausted sleep. She'd woken up about an hour ago, groggy and raw, still feeling the effects of the sweaty erotic dreams which had chased her in sleep…

Beyond grateful that the star player in every one of those dreams was still out of the house, she'd managed to figure out the coffee machine and made herself a cup to enjoy with the view of the sunset from her bedroom.

She'd spotted him coming up the stairs from the dock about twenty minutes ago, his head bowed and his body looking far too buff in a clinging wetsuit, his damp hair dishevelled, the way it had been last night when they'd come in from the storm.

Don't think about last night.

As he'd entered the house, the surge of longing had convinced her to stay well clear of him for the night. Confronting him was pointless— all it would do was make her more aware of the desire that would not die, or more anxious about her predicament, because they clearly weren't going to be going anywhere tonight.

She'd managed to find some crime novels on his bookshelves... They should keep her entertained, and might even contain a fiendishly clever and undetectable way to murder a man in his sleep.

But then she'd heard him calling her to come downstairs... Not calling her, *summoning* her—as if she were an employee instead of a hostage.

Ignoring him had been impossible, and it would have made her seem weak. So she had steeled herself against the inevitable surge of heat and forced herself to remain calm. Or calmish...

But then he'd demanded she cook them both dinner, because—as he'd put it so charmingly—'I don't like freeloaders any more than I like spies.'

That was when she'd reminded him of the sandwich.

'I threw the sandwich in the trash,' he replied now.

What the actual...?

A blush rose up her throat, combining with the surge of temper that she'd been keeping carefully at bay ever since his many hissy fits that morning had threatened to blow her head off.

'You... You...' she stuttered, so shocked at

the sneering tone and the complete lack of gratitude for her titanic effort that morning in taking the high road that the words got stuck in her throat. 'You did *what*?' she blurted out at last.

'I threw it in the trash. Next time you make me a sandwich, don't drown it in mayo. I hate the stuff. And don't leave it sitting on the counter all day, so all that's left of it when I get a chance to eat are its fossilised remains.'

She gasped—she actually gasped—so aghast at his audacity and his total inability to show any appreciation for her effort whatsoever that she was actually struggling to draw a decent breath. *'Next time?'* she spat the words out. 'You have got to be joking. There isn't going to be a next time. I'd be more willing to make a sandwich for my worst enemy than you.'

'I *am* your worst enemy right now, and you still owe me,' he shot back, his tone dripping with sarcasm. 'I've been out all day working my butt off and I'm starving, so a sandwich—even if it were actually edible—isn't going to cut it. Let's see what else you've got,' he finished, before stomping past her.

She gulped, a sudden spurt of panic chipping away at her fortifying fury. 'What do you mean, what else I've got?' she asked.

Although she had a horrid feeling she already knew.

He wasn't kidding about expecting her to cook him supper.

A *hot* supper, with *actual* ingredients, from *scratch*—something that didn't come out of a ready meal container or off a takeaway menu.

He stopped and stared down his nose at her. 'What else you've got in your repertoire of go-to meals. Other than prehistoric sandwiches,' he added.

But the dig didn't even register this time as her panic started to consume her.

But I don't have a repertoire.

It was what she wanted to say. But she couldn't say it because she knew it would make her look pathetic. Because it *was* pathetic.

She didn't know how to cook anything. Not anything complicated. Nothing other than maybe beans on toast, or scrambled egg, or warmed-over soup from a tin. And she was fairly sure that wouldn't cut it with this man any more than her 'fossilised sandwich' had—because he could whip up a pancake batter from scratch and had been a short-order chef in a diner when he was still a teenager.

The truth was, she had no excuse. She should have learned how to cook for herself a long time ago. But she'd avoided learning, avoided even attempting to learn. And the reason for that was even more pathetic.

She hated being in a kitchen and doing any kind of domestic chores because it reminded her of the day she had discovered exactly how much her father disapproved of her...

Not even disapproved of her, really. Because disapproval required some kind of emotional input. And the truth was Aldous James hadn't cared enough about his daughter to put in any emotional effort.

He hadn't disapproved of her. He hadn't even seen her. And the day she had discovered exactly how little he cared had haunted her every day since—whenever she spent any time in a kitchen.

For five years—from the day Ash and her mother had come to live in the servants' quarters at her father's house on Regent's Park West—the kitchen had become a place of solace and sanctuary for Cassie. A place of vibrancy and life and excitement, for good times and good feelings.

Until the day her father had chosen to change all that without telling her.

The heat in her cheeks exploded as she recalled that day in vivid detail.

She had raced down the stairs brimming with exhilaration because it had been the first day of October half-term. She had known Ash would be up early, having her breakfast while Ash's

mother, Angela, put together her father's breakfast tray. Her friend would already be concoct-
ing some marvellous new adventures for them
both for the holiday. Because Ash always came
up with the best adventures.

But it hadn't been only Ash's latest mad plans
that Cassie had been anticipating as she'd shot
down the back stairs in her family's ten-bed-
room Georgian town house—a house that
had felt like a prison to her—a prison full of
ghosts—until Angela had appeared one day in
the staff quarters and introduced Cassie to her
daughter.

*'Sure, you two are about the same age. I
won't mind a bit if you want to come down and
keep Ashling and I company while your father
is busy.'*

She hadn't just been excited about spending
some quality time with her best friend again
after weeks and weeks of boring school, when
they'd only got to see each other for a few hours
a day because of the endless hours of homework
Cassie was set by the posh private school she'd
attended. She'd also been anticipating basking
in the homely atmosphere Angela and Ash had
created ever since they'd come into her life.

She'd loved all of it. The comforting witter-
ing of Angela Doyle's conversations about fair-
ies and crystals and other nonsense, the sound

of Ash's slightly off-key singing as they sang along to her favourite show tunes while sharing the headphones from Ash's MP3 player, the tempting aroma of the scones and breads Angela baked from scratch and the scent of lavender floor polish.

She'd burst through the kitchen door that crisp October day when she was thirteen with the wonderful feeling of belonging, of friendship, bursting in her heart—only to find the room cold and empty and silent.

And Ash's hastily written note on the table telling her they'd been forced to leave.

A cold weight sank into her stomach all over again, joining the sharp twist of inadequacy as she recalled the conversation in her father's study later that day.

'Angela Doyle is no longer in my employ. We don't need a housekeeper any more as you will be boarding at St Bride's after half-term and I can simply eat at my club.'

'But, Father, what about Ashling? She's my best friend.'

'Ashling is a housekeeper's daughter. She is hardly a suitable companion for you.'

Cassie pushed past the recollection, disturbed by the realisation that her father's callous words that day and his blank expression—impatient and vaguely annoyed—still had the power to make the muscles in her stomach clench into a knot.

How pathetic that she could still recall that day in such vivid detail. Especially now, when the last thing she needed was to give Luke Broussard more ammunition.

For goodness' sake, Cassie, get over yourself.

How ridiculous to let the devastation of that day still control her all these years later… Maybe her life had been more colourful with Ash and her mum living in the staff quarters. And, yes, it had been thoughtless and insensitive of her father to wrench them away from her without a thought to how she might react. But to think she had avoided learning to cook because of that one painful memory…?

Seriously, it was beyond pathetic.

Especially when she considered that everything she'd thought she had lost that day had never really been lost at all. Ash was still her best friend. They'd made sure never to lose touch during all those miserable years Cassie had spent at St Bride's. They had been sharing a flat together for the last four years, ever since Cassie had finished uni and begun her career at Temple's as a graduate associate.

It was all good. Give or take the odd bra-less dress debacle and tuxedo *ditzkrieg*.

Cassie cleared her throat.

Except for one glaring problem. She did not have a 'go-to' meal repertoire which she could use to whip up something now and impress Luke Broussard. Not even close. Which meant the only course of action open to her—as her tormentor continued to stare at her with utter contempt—was to bluff. Because she would actually rather die than let him know she had allowed that easily bruised, painfully lonely child to continue to lurk inside her for so long.

'Cook your own supper,' Cassie said, drawing herself up to her full height—which was still a lot shorter than his—and trying to draw on the outrage of a moment ago. 'I'm not your personal chef.'

She swung round to make what she planned to be a dignified and speedy exit.

Too late.

'Not so fast, Miss Priss.' He grasped hold of her elbow to tug her back.

A spike of adrenaline shot up her arm, adding shocking heat to the twist of pain and inadequacy already festering in her belly.

To her horror, instead of accepting her perfectly reasonable rebuttal, Luke Broussard tilted his head to one side, studying her in that strangely unsettling way he had that made her feel totally transparent.

'You can't cook, can you?' he said.

It wasn't a question.

'How do you…?' She stopped, her pulse tripping into overdrive as the weight in her stomach grew to impossible proportions. 'Of course I can,' she said, scrambling to cover the gaffe.

'Uh-huh?' he said. 'Then prove it.'

'I don't have to prove anything to you,' she managed, but she could tell from his expression that the game was up.

'What are you? Some kind of princess?' he said, contempt dripping from his words now. She should have been prepared for it. She wasn't. Especially as she didn't even have anything resembling a decent excuse. The weight in her stomach twisted and throbbed on cue.

'No, it's just… It's not a skill I've ever needed. Particularly…' she said, desperately trying to cover her tracks. Bluffing hadn't worked. Maybe bluster would.

'Why?'

'We had s-staff when I was little, and I went to boarding school.'

She stumbled over the word 'staff', because she'd never thought of Angela as her father's employee. Angela Doyle had been the closest thing she'd ever had to a mother. Which was why she had been devastated when her father had let her go—as well as Ash.

But Luke didn't need to know any of that.

Playing the privileged spoilt princess made her feel stronger, somehow, than the truth… That she'd been a needy, lonely child, looking for affection from people who had been paid to care for her. Angela had never made it seem that way, but that was the reality.

'You had staff…' he said, cursing softly under his breath. 'That's the excuse you've got for not learning a basic life skill?'

'Well, it can't be that basic if I've survived perfectly well without it,' she said.

'Until now,' he said, sounding exasperated with her incompetence. 'I mean, *damn*. What about your mama? Didn't she teach you something? Anything?'

'No, I was only four when she died.'

As soon as the words were out of her mouth she wanted to take them back. Because his eyes darkened and what she saw on his face, instead of distrust or anger or even heat—which seemed to be his go-to emotions where she was concerned—was pity.

'That's tough, *cher.*'

It was the first time he'd used the endearment since discovering Ash's text, and to Cassie's horror the growled condolence had an effect she couldn't mitigate or guard against, brushing over her skin and making her heartbeat slow and her ribs squeeze, cutting off her breathing.

She stiffened and re-inflated her lungs with an effort.

'You're weak, Cassandra, that's your problem.'

Her father's voice slashed across her consciousness. She forced herself to keep breathing past the pain in her chest and the boulder in her throat.

Don't you dare cry—not in front of him. You're just tired and stressed. This is not a big deal.

'Not really. I don't even remember her,' she lied. 'And, anyhow, that's a little sexist, isn't it? To assume my mother would teach me how to cook?' she added, trying to regain at least some of her self-respect and the fighting spirit she'd worked so hard to create over all the years of her father's indifference.

Men like Luke Broussard saw a weakness and exploited it. That was what they did.

Luke shrugged, but his expression didn't change, his clear mossy-green eyes still shadowed. 'I guess it could have been your papa,' he said, the French inflection on the word sounding strangely intimate. 'I just asked because my mama taught me. She always said I needed to know the basics…' He counted them off on his fingers. 'Gumbo, Jambalaya, crawfish étouffée and pancakes.'

'I only know what one of those things even is,' Cassie supplied, stupidly relieved as the knot in her stomach loosened a fraction.

As much as she might want to stand up to him, handling confrontation head-on had never been her strong suit—just ask her father.

Luke swore again, but she felt the knot release a little more. Maybe he despised her, but at least she wasn't going to have to fake any cordon bleu cooking skills now.

Always an upside.

'Well, we've both gotta eat tonight. And I'll be damned if I'm gonna do it all. If you want, I can show you how to cook my mama's Jambalaya?'

Warmth blossomed in the pit of her stomach alongside a burst of astonishment. But then she got a grip and saw the pity still shadowing his eyes.

The off-hand offer wasn't really meant as an olive branch—she totally got that. He was quite possibly only doing it to demonstrate to her exactly how pathetic she was. But somehow she couldn't bring herself to tell him where he could stick his offer.

Unfortunately, she was fairly sure her inability to tell him no wasn't just because she was so hungry she was more than ready to eat anything—even humble pie—but also because darkness was closing in outside the window, and spending the evening with him without having to argue with him would be better than spending it alone in the guest room.

'I think I could probably manage that,' she said cautiously, hating herself a little bit for folding far too easily, but deciding she could always go back to standing up to him tomorrow. Tonight, she was too stressed and exhausted and famished. 'If you tell me exactly what to do.'

The quirk of his lips took on a wicked tilt— and suddenly she was fairly sure he wasn't thinking about cooking any more. Because neither was she.

'Don't worry, I'm real good at giving orders.'

Don't I know it? she thought, but didn't say. Because with the thought came a blast of unhelpful memories about the orders he'd given her the night before, and how much she'd enjoyed obeying them without question.

Way to go, Cassie. Why not turn a catastrophe into a sex-tastrophe? Because this isn't already awkward enough...

'Go grab the bag of crawfish from the freezer,' he said, the teasing glint instantly gone again, 'and then I'll show you how to make Jambalaya.'

She was so relieved that he seemed as disinclined to flirt as she was, that she was halfway across the kitchen before she thought to turn around and ask, 'What does a crawfish look like?'

He paused while grabbing a pan from the rack above the kitchen island, a low chuckle bursting out of his mouth. 'Hell, *cher*, don't you know anything?'

Apparently not. But suddenly not being able to cook didn't seem like her biggest problem, when the rusty rumble of spontaneous laughter rippled over her skin and made the ever-present weight in her stomach start to throb.

Hello, downside, my old friend.

Whose dumb idea was it to give her cooking lessons?

Luke watched Cassandra's forehead crease as she shook the skillet. The sizzle of frying scallions and garlic was doing nothing to mask the smell of his pine shampoo on her hair. She scraped the pan with the spatula.

Oh, yeah, your dumb idea.

'Just tease it,' he said, wrapping his fingers around her wrist to direct her movements.

Her pulse jumped under his thumb and she jolted. The stirring in his groin, which he thought he'd taken care of an hour ago in the mud room shower, hit critical mass. He let go of her wrist as if he'd been burned. Because that

was what it felt like—as if she were a live electrical socket which he couldn't resist jamming
his fingers into.

'That's it…you got it,' he said, regretting his
spur-of-the-moment decision even more as he
got another lungful of her clean scent over the
pungent smell of frying garlic. His burgeoning
erection hardened and he stepped back, far too
aware of the urge to press it into the curve of
her backside.

He cursed silently.

By rights he should be exhausted.

By rights he should have taken care of this
yearning in the shower and during twelve hours
of chores and outdoor pursuits.

By rights he should want to have nothing
whatsoever to do with this woman.

She'd lied and cheated and had intended to
use the connection between them to spy on him
for her boss. So why couldn't he get his hunger
for her under control? And why had the look
on her face when he'd demanded she cook him
supper, then asked her about her mama, torn at
his insides?

When she'd come back from the cellar where
he kept a chest freezer, holding a bag of frozen crawfish aloft like a fisherman with a prize
catch, the smile of accomplishment which had
split her face had hit him square in the chest.

And he'd known he'd made another major error of judgement. Because spending any time with her, let alone teaching her something she should have been taught long ago, was going to be pure torture.

Why did she have to look so hot in Mrs Mendoza's jeans? And why had the truth about her mama made him aware of her fragility instead of her duplicity?

He set about dicing bell peppers and then instructed her on how to sift and rinse the rice and make the broth. All the while trying to persuade himself that he had been played again.

How did he know that the brave, motherless girl act wasn't as much of a con as the forthright, artless sex goddess act of yesterday?

But somehow, as she worked diligently to follow his instructions to the letter and make as little eye contact with him as possible, he couldn't shake the memory of the look of devastating loss which had shimmered in her eyes when he'd harassed her about her cooking skills.

And somehow he knew, even though he wanted to recapture his previous cynicism and harden his attitude towards her, that Cassandra James wasn't that good an actress.

He'd touched a nerve somehow. A nerve he'd never meant to expose. And he couldn't quite bring himself to exploit it.

Picking up the rice she'd sorted, and the sausage he'd fried earlier, he chucked it into the skillet on top of the vegetables.

'Is your mother still alive?' she asked carefully over the sizzling of the food.

'No, she died when I was sixteen,' he said, not only surprised by her decision to break their truce, but also by the pulse of connection he felt. Just because they'd both lost their mothers when they were still kids, it didn't make them friends.

'I'm sorry,' she said. 'She was very beautiful.'

'How would you know?' he asked, pushing his cynicism back to the fore. *Damn*, was she still spying on him?

'I saw a picture of the two of you on your desk,' she said, her forthright expression daring him to make a big deal out of it.

'What were you doing in my office?' he demanded.

'Trying to find a phone charger so I can save my career,' she shot back, but then her gaze softened. 'I'm so sorry for your loss,' she added, and he could see she meant it. 'I didn't see any photos of your father, but I hope—despite his bad reputation—he was still…'

'I never met him,' he lied smoothly. 'After she died I was on my own. But that was the way I wanted it.'

'Then why are you so worried about people

finding out about him?' she asked, her expression open and uncomplicated. 'Surely his reputation can't hurt you? Not after everything you've achieved?'

He swallowed, but the lump of anger in his throat, that was always there when he thought of his father had faded. 'I'm not worried about it any more,' he said, astonished to realise it was true. 'Now, stop snooping and start stirring,' he added, suddenly desperate to change the subject before the compassion in her gaze got to him.

She stiffened at the curtness in his tone, but did as she was told. The recollection of how she'd followed instructions last night, too, sent a shaft of heat through his overworked system. But this time he welcomed it as he set about defrosting the crawfish in the microwave.

He didn't want to care about her loss—didn't want to feel any connection to her grief or recall how much he had needed his own mom growing up, and how much he'd missed her when she was gone.

His mother had been the only person to stand by him through all those years of being despised, being kicked around and treated like dirt because of his old man. He definitely didn't want to think about how much it had hurt when he'd lost her too soon.

But as he peeled the crawfish it reminded

him of how he'd watched his mother doing the same task in their trailer. And the words she'd spoken to chastise and console him.

'Don't go getting yourself into more fights— you hear me? It won't change a thing. All it'll do is give them an excuse to judge you more.'

She'd been right, of course, and eventually he'd listened. But what would it have been like to have none of that guidance, none of that care and compassion when you needed it most, no one to tend you when you were hurting, to teach you what you needed to be taught?

The tightness in his chest increased.

Not the point. She still used you. Just because she lost her mama young, it doesn't make her someone you can trust.

He breathed deep, to calm the pummelling of his heart and the low-grade pulsing in his pants. Leaning closer, he poured the broth into the pan. It spat on the hot metal and made her flushed face glow.

Heat slammed into him again. 'You can stop stirring,' he said.

She dropped the spatula and edged away from him, obviously finely tuned to how volatile his feelings had become—which just made the feeling of connection more acute. *Damn her.*

'It'll take a while to cook now,' he said, placing the lid on the pan so the food could steam.

He glanced her way, taking in the gentle sway of her breasts, which he could detect even under the housekeeper's sweater, and making him far too aware of how much he wanted to cup the plump flesh…

'I'm afraid we're gonna be stuck here together for a couple of days at least,' he murmured.

Her eyebrows rose up her forehead, and the flush on her cheeks intensified, but the argument he'd been expecting didn't come.

'I assume it's unavoidable?' she said.

'Yeah, it is,' he said. Even though it wasn't… entirely.

Truth be told, he could get her back to the mainland sooner rather than later if he was prepared to spend the next couple of days fixing the speedboat's hull. Or, when the cell service came back—which it would—pay to have a mechanic flown out to fix Jezebel…

But he was forcing himself to stick to the plan of action he'd decided on earlier. Why should he ruin his vacation or spend a small fortune just for her convenience?

Plus, keeping her here until the product launch was good insurance.

He knew she was right in what she'd said— his father's sins had never been his. Why should he keep them hidden any longer? Didn't that just give the bastard a power over him that he had never deserved?

His gaze flicked over her breasts and back to her face as the heat continued to pulse in his groin. But just because he still desired her, and she'd made a good point about his old man, it didn't mean he was going to let this attraction get the better of him.

She was watching him with those guarded eyes, and he had the weirdest vision of a young doe bracing itself for the hunter to shoot when she said, 'I'm sorry this happened. I really didn't intend to spy on you…'

She swallowed, and he realised he wanted to take her words at face value.

'I'll be sure to stay out of your way until I can leave,' she added.

'You do that,' he said, annoyed at the pulse of regret he felt when she stiffened at his surly statement. 'If you need food, Mrs Mendoza leaves stuff in the freezer that you can nuke,' he added, to soften the blow while also making it crystal-clear that no more impromptu cooking lessons would be forthcoming. 'I'll shout once this is ready and you can eat in one of the guest rooms,' he finished.

'All right.'

She walked away, and the strange pang in his chest increased. But then she turned back.

'Thanks for teaching me how to make your mother's Jambalaya.'

'Not a problem,' he murmured.

Even though he knew it *was* a problem—*she* was a problem—which he had a bad feeling he now had even less of a clue how to fix.

CHAPTER SEVEN

CASSIE STEPPED OUT through the back door of the housekeeper's annexe wearing the raincoat she'd borrowed from Mrs Mendoza's dwindling supply of clean clothing.

Sun shone off the dew clinging to the ferns and rhododendrons lining the path and burned away the last of the morning mist. After a whole day yesterday spent hiding out in her room, in between sneaked trips to the kitchen to heat up food whenever the coast was clear—which had been most of the time, because Luke seemed to be avoiding her with the same dedication with which she was avoiding him—she was going stir crazy.

She zipped up the raincoat, settled the borrowed backpack on her shoulders and set out along the path which, according to the map, led to a trail that circumnavigated the island.

Worrying about her inability to contact her office—or anyone, for that matter—and how long it might be before she got back to San Francisco, not to mention the job of avoiding her reluctant host and any more too revealing heart-to-hearts at all costs, wasn't helping with her sleep deprivation. Or her stress levels.

She needed to get out of the house. Perhaps she was not the outdoors type, but the only way to take her mind off Luke and the things she'd learned about him two days ago was to fill her time with something else. And a hike was pretty much her only option.

From what she could remember when they'd flown into the bay three nights ago, the island was more than big enough to contain both of them without there being much chance of her bumping into him. She'd managed to find a small guidebook to Oregon's bird life. She would tour the area, scope out the terrain, and see if she could spot some of the birds indigenous to the Pacific Northwest. Because staying holed up in his house all day yesterday had given her far too much time to mull over the conversation they'd had about his childhood.

'After she died I was on my own. But that was the way I wanted it.'

Did he really believe that? She frowned. And why did she care whether he did or not? She'd had no business probing, or offering him advice about a relationship with the father he'd never known, when her relationship with her own father could best be described as barely functional. She couldn't even sort out her own daddy issues, so what made her think she could sort out his?

One thing she did know, though: keeping busy had always kept her sane—especially when she was dealing with a problem outside her control, such as the loneliness she'd fallen into when her father had pushed Ashling and Angela Doyle out of her life without any warning, or the fact that she'd got stranded on a taciturn billionaire's private island and started to delude herself into believing they had something in common, when they clearly did not.

Avoidance had always been her great go-to strategy. So, having stuffed the backpack with the bird book, some energy bars, a bottle of water, a map and a pair of binoculars, she was all set to make the best of things. Plus, physical exhaustion might help with her sleep issues.

Wisps of moisture still clung to the headland as the path meandered past the dock and into the forest. She breathed in, the air so crisp it hurt her lungs. A bracing walk and some bird-spotting would do her the world of good. Not that she knew the first thing about bird-spotting, but how hard could it be?

* * *

Two hours later Cassie wheezed to the top of another steep incline on the cliff path. She bent over to catch her breath, stunned again by the startling natural beauty of Sunrise Island… And by how chronically unfit she was. Who knew two spin classes a year weren't enough to prepare you for a ten-mile hike?

After drawing in several deep breaths of the clean air, she stood to admire another staggering view.

The outcropping of volcanic rock she stood on formed a natural archway, revealing a hidden cove eighty feet below her. The black sand beach, scattered with driftwood from the recent storm, curved around the headland, edged by the vivid green of the towering redwoods and pines on one side and a sheer rock face on the other. Her breathing slowed and her heart swelled. The scent of salt water carried on the breeze and tempered the heat of the midday sunshine.

She pulled the map out of her pack and located her position.

Pirates' Cove.

An apt name, given who owned it.

A jolt of awareness took her tired body unawares.

Not thinking about him, remember…?

She pushed the unhelpful thought to one side as she spotted a bird offshore, its large wingspan holding it aloft on the sea air. She scrambled to dig the bird book and the binoculars out of the backpack, then focussed the binoculars on the magnificent creature.

Was that an eagle or a hawk?

She flicked through the book to the pages she'd dog-eared during the many breaks she'd taken, to give her unconditioned legs some downtime in between the more strenuous climbs. She studied the pictures. Then lifted the binoculars again. Surely it was an eagle? Wasn't it too big to be a hawk?

Her heart beat a giddy tattoo as the bird swooped straight down into the waves, then climbed again with a small silver fish clamped in its beak. As it skimmed above the surface of the water, carrying its prey back to its nest, she followed its progress, marvelling at its speed and dexterity, but then she saw it fly over something in the water.

For one moment she thought it might be a seal, but then the dark shape ploughing through the waves morphed into something sleeker and more defined.

A swimmer in a wetsuit.

Luke.

She focussed the binoculars on him, her gaze

fixed on the solitary figure, and all the thoughts she'd been keeping so carefully at bay during her gruelling hike flooded back.

He seemed oblivious to the violent action of the waves as he moved towards the shore, battling against the retreating tide, each tumble of surf dragging him back out to sea. He kept heading in the same direction, unfazed, uncompromising, ruthless, resilient and totally focussed on his goal.

Was he in danger? What if he was drowning and she was just watching?

The visceral fear faded, though, before she had a chance to act on it, as he found his footing and stood in thigh-deep water.

Her heart pulsed hard as she thought of the sixteen-year-old boy, left alone but unafraid. Determined to survive and make a staggering success of his life, despite what must have been impossible odds.

The tide continued to buffet him as he made his way through the rolling waves, but he seemed oblivious to its energy, arriving on the sand moments later undaunted. His dark hair lay plastered to his head, curling slightly around his neck, and his tanned face was burnished by the sun as he stood with his legs apart, his hands fisted on his hips, the clinging suit creating a powerful silhouette. He closed his eyes to tilt his head back and the sun gilded his features once more, making him for one fanciful moment look like a sea god, confident in his ability to command the ocean and win.

Cassie's breathing slowed, and then accelerated as relief that he was okay, that he was safe, sent a well of emotion through her tired body.

He looked magnificent. Powerful and intimidating in his masculine beauty. The yearning which was never far away flowed through her again. The same giddy exhilaration which had blindsided her in San Francisco was somehow more intense now, and even more overwhelming—despite twenty-four hours of avoidance and several more hours of his disapproval.

He shifted, twisting his arm up his back to grab the strap which dangled down. He tugged the zip tab to peel off the wetsuit.

Look away. Look away now.

She was invading his privacy—and only making the agitation she'd been trying to control the last couple of days worse again. But she couldn't seem to force herself to lower the binoculars…couldn't stop looking.

Her gaze was riveted to the taut contours of muscle and sinew as he freed his arms from the suit. She absorbed every inch of exposed skin, her fingers trembling as they tightened on the binoculars. She studied the curls of hair around his nipples that meandered in a line through his abs. She didn't move—couldn't move—as he shoved the wetsuit off his hips and down his legs. Her gaze clung to the tensed muscles of his flanks, sprinkled with hair, then honed in on the dark thicket at his groin. The tattoo which curved over his hip pointed her to his sex, which hung limp but still looked remarkably impressive despite his cold swim.

A hot weight sank like a fireball between her tired thighs and made her own sex throb.

But it wasn't just the memory of their intense physical connection that first night which had her throat thickening.

It was the memories of the man she had met in San Francisco—playful, demanding, flirtatious, so into her before he'd turned against her. The man who had wanted her as desperately as she'd wanted him. Who hadn't judged her, hadn't despised her.

Why did her throat hurt so much as she remembered that man now? The man she'd thought she'd glimpsed again when he'd offered to teach her how to make Jambalaya and had shared things she never would have expected him to share with her?

Why should she still be moved by that man when she wasn't even sure he was real?

Kicking the suit away, Luke picked up a towel

resting on a piece of driftwood and began to dry himself. Still Cassie watched, unable to deny herself the pleasure and the pain of those memories and the glorious sight of her first lover.

The fact that Luke Broussard would always be her first lover shouldn't really have any great significance. That was what she'd told herself at the time. What she still wanted to believe. But how could it not?

She swallowed, aware of raw desire and the sting of tears. She had to stop looking—had to walk away. She had a long trek back to the house and she needed to get there before he did and get a grip on her wayward emotions. Which really made no sense whatsoever. What had happened between them that first night wasn't going to happen again. He'd made that abundantly clear. And anyway she didn't want it to happen again.

Did she?

Hadn't the emotional fallout from that mistake already been devastating enough?

But just as she made the decision to stop looking his head jerked up, his gaze locking on the exact spot where she stood. For a second she stood frozen, still staring back at him through the binoculars. Caught. Trapped. Unable to escape from that hard, magnetic gaze. Then she lowered the binoculars and scrambled back, snapped out of her trance by panic and guilty knowledge.

She hid for a few precious seconds, long enough to get her breath back, before she finally she got up the guts to take another look.

The spurt of terror and guilt—and adrenaline—faded as she watched him head to a pile of clothing and dress himself with slow deliberation. Without the binoculars he was little more than a speck on the landscape... He couldn't possibly have spotted her all the way up here, unless he had better eyesight than the eagle.

But the relief that he hadn't caught her spying on him like a besotted schoolgirl didn't last long as she headed back into the forest.

Why had she stared at him like that? What was wrong with her? Where was Cassie the boring rule-follower when she needed her? Because she did not need that wild woman back again. Not in any shape or form. That woman had caused her more than enough trouble already...

So, Cassandra James is full of...

Luke cursed under his breath.

She'd lied to him. Hadn't she promised she'd steer clear of him? And here she was spying on him again.

Even before he'd seen the tell-tale glimmer of sunlight reflected on glass giving away her position—probably shining off the lenses of his own binoculars—he'd felt the zap of awareness on his chilled skin.

How long had she been standing there? And what the hell had she been doing? Other than getting an eyeful of him naked...

Luke tugged on his jeans and buttoned his fly—not easy as that prickle of awareness arrowed down.

Pirates' Cove was his sanctuary, and she'd invaded it. His cold morning swim was the only way he had to contain and control the hunger which was still driving him nuts.

And she'd ruined that too, now.

But alongside the burst of anger and frustration had been the rush of something worse when he'd spotted the flash of light and realised she was watching him. Something giddy and light-headed and kind of demented, which he now recognised as...

Anticipation.

What the hell?

He swore again, viciously. Infuriated with himself as much as her.

He'd caught her spying on him. And instead of being furious, which he had every right to be, for one split second he'd actually been *pleased*.

Was he some kind of glutton for punishment now? Even when he'd been a teenager, treated like dirt by girls he'd thought liked him, he had never been a sucker. He'd stifled his need to be accepted, to be liked, and got over himself. And over them. They'd never really hurt him because he'd never let them.

No one's approval was worth losing your dignity over, or your pride. If the girls he made out with at night didn't want to acknowledge him in the daylight, they could go right to hell. He was in charge of his own destiny now.

He couldn't even remember their names any more, and their faces were just a hazy memory. He'd never had any trouble moving on from those long-ago betrayals... Even as a sex-starved, untried kid, denied the one thing every kid yearned for in high school: acceptance.

But even as he congratulated himself on his ability to preserve his dignity back then, another voice and another memory beckoned.

His mama, her head high as they walked past those guys who'd always sat in front of Cunningham's Deli, holding his hand too tightly while the wolf whistles followed them down the sidewalk.

'If you can put out for a felon, honey, why don't you put out for me?'

'How about I give you some sugar, sweet thing? You ain't going to be getting none from Gino for another five to ten.'

His fingers curled into fists.

How he'd hated those men, and the way they'd spoken to his mama—as if she were a piece of meat instead of a human being. But none of them had been the man he'd hated most of all.

'He doesn't give a damn about us, Mama. When are you going to figure that out?'

The memory of the feel of his mother's open palm slashing across his face made his cheek sting all over again, and his chest tightened with the same impotent, futile rage that had tortured him as a teenager.

'Don't you disrespect your papa. He loves us. And when he gets out he's gonna take care of us again.'

It was the one thing his mama had always been dead wrong about. Gino Leprince hadn't loved either one of them. If he had he wouldn't have ended up in the penitentiary, doing time for grand theft auto and aggravated assault—without a thought for the heavily pregnant seventeen-year-old girl he'd left behind.

But Celestine Broussard Dupuis had been too starry-eyed, too sweet and gullible and idealistic to see it.

He shook the memory loose, felt the shudder of long forgotten anger racking his body replaced by irritation.

Jesus, where had that come from?

He wasn't a sap, like his mom.

He had loved her dearly, but he'd always been aware of Celestine Dupuis's faults. The most glaring of which had been to mix up sex with emotion—to think that making love with a guy meant he cared about you. That he would protect you and provide for you.

Love had been a trap for her, and ultimately for him, because it had anchored them both in a place where no one had respected them thanks to the crimes of someone else.

It had been the only upside of growing up as the son of the town's biggest screw-up—learning to be cynical about the starry-eyed hogwash called love that robbed you of your common sense, your dignity and self-respect.

Had his conversation with Cassandra shaken all that loose again? Because if it had, he had even more reason to be mad with her.

He flung his towel and his wetsuit over his shoulder and headed round the point to where he'd anchored his kayak.

He shoved the boat off the rocks and jumped in.

Cassandra James had messed with his head two days ago and now she was doing it again.

Well, that ends now.

He'd given her space and she'd taken advantage of that. Coming out here and spying on him when she'd promised not to. Why was he even surprised she hadn't stuck to her word? It was just one more example of how he couldn't trust her.

He sliced the paddle into the water, picking up speed as the kayak rode over the surf and caught the tide.

He could see a new storm gathering, and the sun was starting to sink behind the point. She had a long walk back to the house—and once she got there he would be waiting.

CHAPTER EIGHT

CASSIE TOOK THE steps two at a time, with the long shadows chasing her all the way to the back door of the imposing wood and glass structure.

She pressed her forehead against the cold steel, stupidly pleased to have got to the house before the last of the light faded on the horizon. The sun had set less than five minutes ago, but even so the familiar vice around her chest tightened.

She forced herself to even her breathing. *Grow up. You're fine...you're safe...you're back now. You did not have to spend a night lost in the forest.*

She had always had an idiotic fear of the darkness, and had been forced to sleep with a light on at night ever since she was a little girl.

Except when...

The recollection of strong arms cradling her, a hard body cocooning her against the storm, protecting her after dark, pushed against her consciousness… And the disturbing truth occurred to her for the first time.

Except when I fell asleep in Luke Broussard's arms.

She blew out a breath, pushed the unhelpful thought away.

Wonderful, Cassie. Just what you need to make you feel even more pathetic.

She rubbed her open palms down her jeans, inhaled and exhaled several more times.

She'd got lost on her way back from Pirates' Cove—probably because she hadn't been able to think about anything except Luke Broussard and his naked body.

Her map-reading skills were rusty at best—when was the last time she'd been outside of London, let alone hiking in an Oregon island wilderness?—so it had taken her several wrong turns before she'd finally found the coastal path that would take her back to Luke's house.

But she'd still been a good two miles away—according to the map—when she'd noticed the sun starting to dip ominously towards the horizon and the wind beginning to whip away the last of the day's warmth.

Suddenly getting caught eyeballing Luke Broussard's very delectable naked body had been the least of her worries…

She pressed the code into the control panel

so she could enter the house, and stepped inside just as the drizzle which had soaked through her clothing an hour ago turned into fat drops of rain. The metal door slid closed behind her, shutting out the beginning of the storm. Her tense shoulders finally relaxed.

She shivered, stripping off her damp sweater and boots, feeling the underfloor heating sending some much-needed warmth through her tired, overwrought system.

The lights in the entranceway emphasised the gathering darkness outside and her heart did a panicked two-step. The utter exhaustion—both mental and physical—which she had been holding at bay with sheer force of will for the last mile of her hike began to make her over-used muscles ache, and the tension headache at the base of her skull turn from a whisper into a shout.

No more indiscriminate hiking. Or extra-curricular bird watching. Especially not less than three hours before dark and/or in the vicinity of Pirates' Cove.

To avoid Luke from now on she would have to venture out with extreme caution.

She dropped her backpack, headed through the mud room, and flicked on the lights before taking the steps down to the basement.

Her hollow stomach howled in protest. She

needed food. A hot shower. Some painkillers and bed. In that order. At least tonight she shouldn't have any trouble sleeping.

She rummaged through the chest freezer for one of Mrs Mendoza's ready meals and found a vegetable lasagne in a glass container. Carrying the dish under her arm, she headed back upstairs and scanned the dark open-plan living space.

Only the lights in the kitchen were on. The clenched muscles in her stomach relaxed.

Empty. Luke must still be out and about.

She'd been more than ready to forgo the first part of her To Do list and starve herself until morning if she had found Luke already there. She might be famished, but she did not want to face him tonight. She simply didn't have the mental bandwidth to deal with his overbearing presence when she was already exhausted and perilously close to tears.

Not only did Luke Broussard have the ability to look right into her soul and discover all her secrets without even trying, there was no way on earth she wanted to risk seeing him with the vision still in her head of him naked and gorgeous and indomitable in Pirates' Cove.

The kitchen's lighting glowed on the clean granite work surfaces. She tiptoed into the quiet space, finding the fierce patter of the rain almost soothing as she placed the container on one of the surfaces without making a sound and set about programming the microwave.

She'd heat up the pasta dish and head upstairs to her room with a plate. Safe for another night.

'Sneaking around comes real natural to you, doesn't it?' a deep voice purred from the darkness.

Cassie let out a high-pitched squeak and swung round so fast the lasagne dish launched off the counter like a missile. The sound of glass shattering blasted away the last of her calm.

She steadied herself against the countertop as Luke Broussard's tall, broad and uniquely intimidating silhouette rose from one of the sunken sofas in the living area.

She gulped in a few desperate breaths, then pressed her palm to her chest to steady her rampaging heartbeat and control the vice now tightening around her ribs with the force of a starving anaconda. How long had he been lying in wait, ready to scare the bejesus out of her?

'Are you actually trying to kill me?' she managed—not easy with the adrenaline now pumping round her body at warp speed.

He stepped into the light.

Heat powered through her exhausted system. He'd showered and shaved since she'd left him in the cove. And put on a few more clothes. *Thank goodness.*

Unfortunately, the black cashmere jumper did nothing to disguise the sleek musculature of the chest she'd been admiring four hours, five miles and one major coronary episode ago.

Look away from the six-pack.

She forced her gaze to his face and noticed a muscle tensing in his jaw. And the flat, disapproving line of his lips. Apparently he hadn't been lying in wait to scare her for a laugh.

She should be grateful that he hadn't enjoyed seeing her learn how to levitate, but somehow she wasn't—because his displeasure was having a far more devastating effect.

'I'm not trying to kill you,' he said. 'But if I did, I reckon a judge would consider it justifiable homicide.'

He ground out the words, and it occurred to her that Luke Broussard was absolutely furious. Possibly even more furious than he had been when he'd read Ash's text two days ago.

Just as she was trying to figure out what she could possibly have done, he supplied her with the answer.

'You get a good enough look this afternoon?'

Shame combined with panic, and the inappropriate shaft of heat climbing up her torso.

'You *saw* me?' she blurted out, before she realised how incriminating that sounded.

He stepped closer, making her even more aware of her height disadvantage in the woolly socks. The subtle scent of pine soap filled her senses and she saw the glint of fury turn the mossy green of his irises to emerald fire.

'Uh-huh,' he said, almost casually.

But she could see what the semblance of control was costing him in the rigid line of his jaw and the vein pounding in his temple.

'Next time you're going to use binoculars to check out my junk, don't stand facing the sun.'

'I… I wasn't checking out your junk… Precisely…' she said, but even she could hear the weakness in her denial. And feel the tell-tale blush warming her cheeks.

'Then what *were* you doing… *Precisely?*' he snarled.

'I was watching an eagle… Or… Or possibly a hawk.' She hesitated, hopelessly flustered. 'I'm really not sure what it was.'

Shut up, Cassie. Rambling incoherently about the bird you couldn't identify before you got fixated on his junk is not going to make you look any less guilty.

'I couldn't find it in the book,' she added, so jittery now that she was incapable of obeying even her own instructions. 'But it was big… *Very* big.'

Her gaze drifted south, entirely of its own accord, then shot back up so fast it was a miracle she didn't break her neck. The blush exploded.

The muscle in his jaw remained as rigid as pre-cast steel. And about as forgiving. 'Why did you track me to the cove? And why were you spying on me there?'

The questions sliced out on a grim murmur of suspicion.

'I didn't track you to the cove. I didn't know you would be there. And I wasn't spying on you.' She fought back, trying not to see all his naked beauty in her mind's eye, but guilty heat glowed on her face regardless.

His eyes narrowed, but then his jawline relaxed, his lips quirking in an arrogant smile that only made her feel more insecure… And volatile.

'Damn…you got a kick out of it, didn't you?'

'I… I don't know what you mean…' she said, but the flush had become radioactive.

'You know, for a corporate spy you're a real crummy liar, Cassandra,' he said.

He stepped closer, crowding her personal space, making her more and more aware of the heat flowing straight to her core and turning her heartbeat so frantic her tired limbs became animated. Energised. A flash of lightning from outside blinded her for a moment, and electrified the sexual tension already sparking between them.

'If you want sex, why don't you just say so?' he growled, the low, husky tone of his voice both provocation and promise. 'No need to sneak around and spy on me. I can't think of a better way to pass the time now we both know exactly where we stand.'

The spark leapt and sizzled, searing her nerve-endings, burning down to her core. But she jerked back a step, her bottom hitting the counter, even as her body clamoured for her to get closer, to take him up on his insulting offer.

She couldn't give in to this yearning again. However powerful, however intoxicating. Not after everything he had accused her of. She had to control the chemistry, the yearning, or she would be lost.

'I don't want sex from you—not any more,' she said.

'You're lying,' he said, so confident, so arrogant, so sure.

'No, I'm not,' she said, but the denial came out on a shattered sob, daunted rather than decisive.

How did he do that? How did he make her want him when she knew she shouldn't?

She lifted her hands, palms out, determined to shove him away, to preserve what little was left of her dignity. But just as her palms flattened on his broad chest a lightning flash and a deafening crash of thunder plunged the house into darkness.

She gasped, blinked, but the black veil was so impenetrable it grabbed her by the throat and yanked her down into a bottomless abyss.

Fear thundered through her veins, weakening her knees and catapulting her heart into her mouth.

She couldn't see, couldn't feel, couldn't breathe.

A whimper escaped. Was that her? How could it be? It sounded like a trapped animal a thousand miles away.

Panic consumed her, turning her into a frightened child, cowering, terrified…and so, so alone…

Until her fingers acknowledged the warm, solid wall she touched and the strong, steady beat of a heart.

The urge to cling to the only human thing in the darkness overwhelmed her. She threw her arms around the broad body, cowered against its strength, folding into herself, fear choking her.

'Please…' she begged, taking great gulping

breaths of the clean pine scent as she tried to escape the terror chasing her.

'Cassandra… It's okay, it's just a power outage,' Luke said, concerned by the choking sound and the whimpering cries coming from this woman who had been turning him on to the point of madness one minute—he'd found her guilty, outraged expression as captivating as every other damn thing about her—and then literally collapsed into his arms the next.

As soon as the lights had cut out.

The rush of shock as her whimpers echoed in the darkness transformed into the swift rush of compassion and Luke wrapped his arms around her trembling body, aware of her nails scraping at his back in desperation.

'Shh… It's okay, I've got you,' he murmured.

Her fingers released their death grip, but still she seemed to be curled into him, her body racked by violent shudders. Was she even aware of his presence?

He sank his face into the rain-soaked, citrus-scented hair that haloed around her head and stifled the jolt of desire. How could she be driving him nuts one second…and be so defence-less the next?

That desire shamed him now—the way it had

in the cove, when he'd spotted her watching him. But for very different reasons.

He'd wanted to goad her, he realised. Wanted to make her as angry and frustrated as he was about the chemistry that would not die when he'd found her sneaking into the kitchen.

And he'd succeeded.

But that impulse had gone south pretty quickly. Because he'd seen the same shocked arousal, the same vicious awareness in her eyes, that had tormented him for days.

And then the lights had gone out and she had retreated somewhere he couldn't follow.

All he could do was hold her until she found herself again.

He wanted to deny her sudden switch from hot, aggravating woman to terrified child— wanted to dismiss it as another trick, another game, another act to garner his sympathy or his co-operation. But she'd never tried to elicit his sympathy before. She'd stood up to him, even offering him comfort when he hadn't asked for it.

'Please don't leave me.'

The hoarse plea pierced through the last of his cynicism.

'I… I can't be alone…not in the darkness,' she added.

Her voice was so small and scared it cruci-
fied him.

'I won't,' he said, finding her face in the darkness, tracing his thumbs over her cheeks. Moisture coated his fingertips, the tears almost as
shocking as her fear. 'Just hang on. The emer-
gency generator will kick in any second.'

He'd wanted her at his mercy—wanted her
to admit she was as tortured by the relentless
desire as he was, as desperate, as close to the
edge... But having her in his arms like this,
so vulnerable, so terrified, so dependent, did
something to him.

None of it good, all of it disturbing.

They stood together for seconds which felt
like hours as he willed the lights to come on,
aware of the shivers still racking her body.

Sympathy and sadness assaulted him. What
the hell had happened to her, to make her so
afraid?

At last the lights flickered back on and the
sound of the rain died to a soft patter. The storm
had passed as quickly as it had come. But the
storm of emotion gripping his chest continued
to bite as she shifted out of his arms.

Blinking against the bright, brittle light, she
turned away and braced her hands on the countertop, holding herself together with a force of
will he had to admire, even as he watched her

try to shove the last of her fear back into the shadows.

'I'm sorry,' she murmured, as if there was something to apologise for. 'I need to go to bed.'

He should let her go. Whatever had just happened, it wasn't his concern. But as she passed him, hightailing it towards the staircase, his hand reached out of its own accord to curl around her bicep.

'Hold on.'

She stopped instantly, her shudder of reaction almost as disturbing as his surge of desire. He forced it down. Again.

'Please, I just...' She stumbled over her words, her head bowed, her humiliation so complete it made his ribs hurt. 'I'm sorry,' she said again, sounding so hopeless that the drawing sensation in his chest cinched tight.

He tucked a knuckle under her chin, lifted her face to his. 'What have you got to be sorry about?' he asked, because suddenly he wanted to know.

The shattered look in her eyes, before she could mask it, turned the golden brown to a rich caramel. She looked away, the glow on her cheeks highlighting the reddened tracks of her tears.

He could see her exhaustion.

He hadn't noticed it earlier, because he'd been

so mad—about everything. But he could see it now, in the weary line of her shoulders, the smudged shadows under her eyes, that bone-jarring shudder when she sighed. So she hadn't been getting any more sleep than he had these last couple days…

'I'm sorry for making such a ridiculous scene.'

She raised her head, the direct stare somehow brave and bold, a valiant attempt to deny her obvious fatigue and the remnants of her anxiety attack.

'I don't want you to think I'm weak, because I'm not,' she added. 'That was just a…a blip. I'm not used to being anywhere that gets so dark at night.'

He found his lips softening at the prim, carefully chosen words, the unconvincing defence. He was captivated, even though he didn't want to be. And relieved that whatever had been terrifying her had been conquered.

Part of him wanted to ask where the 'blip' had *really* come from. What had caused it? Because her explanation was garbage. People didn't react with that level of fear and panic just because they normally lived in a metropolis with a lot of light pollution. What he'd just witnessed was a fairly major phobia was his guess. One she'd somehow managed to keep hidden the first night they'd been together.

How come she'd been okay in the darkness when she was tucked against his body?

He sliced off the thought and stopped himself from asking the question burning in his gut. Increasing the intimacy which was already making his chest hurt would not be a smart move. But somehow, even though he knew he should let her leave, he couldn't seem to loosen his grip on her arm.

His lips quirked and she stiffened.

'What exactly is so amusing?' she snapped. The prickly tone dispelled the last of shadows in her eyes, easing the pressure on his chest.

He let go of her arm, enjoying her show of strength. 'That's gotta be the dumbest thing you've ever said to me,' he replied truthfully. 'Whatever you are, you're not weak.'

Her eyebrows rose up her forehead and he could see the observation had surprised her? Why?

'Okay...well, thanks,' she said, her tone a fascinating mixture of embarrassment and indignation.

He was glad. Because the broken child was finally gone, replaced by the smart, forthright woman whose armour was almost as beautiful to him as the furious light in her eyes which had added streaks of gold to the rich caramel.

His gaze drifted down, entirely of its own accord, and snagged on the front of her T-shirt, where her breasts rose and fell, full and high and untethered. The nipples were clearly visible, puckered into hard peaks beneath the worn cotton of the Portland State logo of the shirt, which he was pretty sure he'd seen a few times on his fifty-something housekeeper.

Funny…that old T-shirt had never looked hot on Mrs Mendoza.

He raised his gaze with an effort, and the flush of indignation on her cheeks did nothing to stem the renewed pulse of desire.

So he went with it.

Desire he understood—it made sense, unlike the pressure in his chest, which still hadn't disappeared.

'Did you get a good enough look?' she demanded, but even he could hear the husky tone under the snark.

She wanted to be offended. But she wasn't. She was turned on.

'Not as good as the look you got this afternoon,' he shot back, rising to the challenge, glad to take the opportunity to meet her on her own terms. 'Seems to me, we're not even close to being even,' he added, unable to resist the provocative statement.

Her expression flashed with the same heat he could feel building in his groin. Hot blood flooded through his system, rich and fluid and familiar, burning everything in its path.

So what else was new?

'Fine,' she announced.

Then she reached down, gripped the hem of his housekeeper's old T-shirt and dragged it up and over her head. She flung it over her shoulder. Her bare breasts bounced, and the sight of ripe reddened nipples, the scent of firm soft flesh, turned the heat in his abdomen to raw fire.

'How's that?' she demanded. 'Are we even yet?'

He swore as his erection thickened so fast it hurt.

Jesus, she was so damn perfect. So exquisite... Her sweet flesh was as soft and succulent as he remembered it. He looked his fill, then lifted his head and saw the same desperate passion that was turning his sex to iron reflected in her eyes.

'Not even close,' he gritted out, then reached to glide his thumb under one plump, puckered nipple.

She gave a shattered gasp and he gripped her

hips, dragged her close to lift her. She wrapped her arms round his shoulders and plunged fingers as needy and desperate as his into his hair.

The pure, heady rush of adrenaline made his arms shake. She slanted her mouth across his and he devoured her moan of surrender.

To hell with it. What were they waiting for? They both wanted this... Both needed this...

He thrust his tongue past her open lips, feeding the heat, and explored the recesses of her mouth, starved for the taste of her after two never-ending days and sleepless nights.

He spied the best available horizontal surface—a couch—and headed towards it with her in his arms, determined to get the rest of her naked before he lost what was left of his mind.

He couldn't wait one more minute to bury himself deep inside that tight, wet heat once more. And to forget about everything but making her scream with pleasure.

This is insane. This is madness.

The thoughts surged into Cassie's head as she gripped Luke's cheeks and sucked on his invading tongue. Then surged right back out again as she welcomed everything he had to give her and demanded more.

Ravenous, desperate, frantic.

Not weak. Not sad. Not alone.

Strong and in command of her own pleasure at last.

He tasted so good, so right. The staggering pain and humiliation of her fear was replaced with hot, unstoppable desire as she clamped her legs around his hips and felt the hard, thick ridge of his erection rubbing against the melting spot between her thighs.

She could have this—could have him. Anything to finally destroy the last of that pitiable, frightened child who had been so exposed, so vulnerable, only moments before.

She didn't want him to think of her like that.

She wanted him to know her like this.

She needed to take the power back, to own it again. The way she had never been able to before him.

He dumped her on the sofa and she shivered—not from the cold, but from the staggering rush of sensations already battering her body, waking it up and making it crave. She resisted the urge to cover herself from his searing gaze as it raked over her.

'Fire on,' he murmured as he stripped off his sweater and threw it away.

Flames leapt to life in the firepit, gilding his tensed muscles in an orange glow, highlighting the dark curls of hair arrowing down to his groin.

She watched transfixed as he undid his belt, stripped off the black jeans and boxer shorts. His erection sprang up, taunting her, tempting her. His penis was longer and thicker than it had been that afternoon, and even more magnificent. The flames from the firepit seemed to lick at her sex, where the throbbing pulse was swelling the sensitive nerve-endings.

'Lose the pants, Cassandra,' he demanded, and the gruff murmur reminded her of how his voice had dragged her out of the abyss minutes before.

'Shh... It's okay, I've got you.'

She blinked, shuddered, and then jerked into action, ruthlessly trying to contain the warmth swelling in her chest.

Don't think about that.

She scrambled to undo the borrowed jeans, shoving them down her legs, taking one woolly sock with them in her haste, frantic to banish the foolish, misguided emotions.

Still about sex. All about sex. Nothing more.

'Now let's lose the panties,' he added, his gruff chuckle reverberating at her core as he hooked his fingers in the waistband and tugged the lace down her legs.

She lifted her bottom to help him, shaking uncontrollably when he flung her panties away and knelt between her legs. He cradled her bare bottom in large palms, sending sensation reeling, and then leant forward to capture one turgid nipple between his teeth.

She bucked off the sofa cushions. His soft nip was like touching a live wire to her breast as sensation slammed down to her core. He feasted on each tortured peak, tugging and tasting and tempting, licking and sucking, then blazed a trail down her belly to blow on the curls of her sex.

She moaned, gasped, propped herself up on her elbows to watch as he parted the wet folds with his thumbs and feasted.

She threw her head back as the focussed attention of his tongue, so devious, so perfect, so sure, made an inferno rip through her.

The orgasm hit with staggering speed and intensity, slamming into her like a freight train. And she flew, remembering the flight of that eagle...soaring over the waves.

As she came down, floating in afterglow, his dark shadow rose over her, his broad shoulders blocking out the orange glow from the firepit. But she wasn't scared any more. She was alive.

She held on to his shoulders, widened her knees to cradle his hips. She needed him to plunge deep and take away the shudder of emotion, that raw feeling of connection.

'I don't have a condom,' he said, his voice strained.

'I wear a contraceptive patch,' she managed, never more grateful for the period pains which had blighted her life for so many years before she'd found the solution.

'I'm clean,' he said. 'I get a test each year for my insurance and I've never gone bareback… before now.'

It took her dazed mind a moment to work out that there was a question in his statement. 'You're my…' She stopped dead, realising she had almost revealed the truth of their first night. 'I haven't slept with anyone for a while. Not since college,' she added trying to make the lie convincing.

'Yeah?' he said.

He tilted his head, considering, and she thought for one horrendous moment she'd been busted. But then his expression became fierce.

'Good to know.'

His fingers firmed on her hips and the huge head of his erection butted her sex. She had a moment to register the self-satisfied tone, and a moment more to panic that she might have exposed herself again, but then every thought flew out of her head as he pressed home.

He surged deep, filling her to the hilt. Then

he began to move. Rocking out, surging back, rolling his hips to conquer every part of her.

Her surge of emotion combined with the shock of sensation. Sharpening, twisting, torturing…

Her shattered sobs matched his deep grunts, her thundering heartbeat echoing in her chest as they moved together in blissful unison. The wave gathered and built like a tsunami this time, so much bigger and bolder than before.

Reaching down, he found the heart of her pleasure, his touch triggering a massive release. The wave barrelled through her and sent her soaring into the stratosphere. She flew free for what felt like an eternity, her body shimmering with bliss. Then collapsed, exhausted and spent, back to earth.

Luke braced his hands on the sofa cushions to stop himself crushing her. He eased out of her tight sheath, grunting as her muscles gripped him, massaging him through the last vicious throes of his orgasm. And hers.

He let out a ragged breath and touched his forehead to hers. 'That was intense,' he said, in what had to be the understatement of the century.

'Hmmm…' she said, her eyes closed, her voice barely a murmur.

He forced himself to lift off her and sit up, suddenly raw and confused. For a moment he'd thought she'd been about to say she had been a virgin after all, and something brutally possessive and protective had surged through him— was still surging through him. Which made no damn sense.

He perched on the edge of the sofa, then glanced over his shoulder to watch her. She rolled away from him, tucked her hands under her cheek and settled into the couch cushions, her naked body given a golden sheen by the light from the firepit.

A few moments later he detected the steady rise and fall of her ribs.

She'd crashed out on him.

A part of him figured he should probably be annoyed she'd dismissed him so easily, but as he studied her—the delectable curve of her bare butt, the elegant line of her spine, the tangle of hair down her back—he couldn't muster much indignation.

If the orgasm had shattered him, it had destroyed her.

Standing, he dragged his boxers back on, far too aware of the renewed pulsing in his groin. But no way were they doing that again tonight, or it would probably kill them both.

A wry smile tugged at his lips, despite the

unsettling direction of his thoughts. After three days of hard physical activity and very little sleep, was it any surprise that he was ready to face-plant after finally addressing the sexual tension that had tormented him? Why should she be any different? That was all this was. Nothing to see here.

He tugged on his sweater, then found a throw rug on the opposite couch to cover her.

But after tucking the soft blanket around her naked body he heard the distant rumble of thunder from the retreating storm. He couldn't leave her alone down here. What if the lights went out again and she woke in the dark?

The tension in his groin moved up to constrict around his heart.

'Ah, to hell with it...' he murmured, then hunkered down and scooped her into his arms, wrapped in the throw.

'Mmm...' she said, groggy and dazed, but then she shifted to snuggle against his chest, as trusting and defenceless as a child.

His heart bobbed as he toted her towards the staircase. 'Come on, Cassandra, let's go to bed.'

He reached the mezzanine, but instead of heading down the hallway towards the guest bedroom she'd been using for the last two days, he walked into the master bedroom.

She wasn't his responsibility... But he didn't ever want to see her fall apart that way again.

He laid her gently on his bed, still covered in the throw rug. One of her feet peeked out of her cocoon and hung over the edge of the mattress. She was wearing one hiking sock.

He frowned, mesmerised and stupidly touched by the sight.

Just a sock, man, get real.

He tugged the dangling sock off, then tucked her slender foot back under the blanket and headed to the bathroom for a cold shower.

When he returned to the bedroom she hadn't moved a single muscle, so deeply asleep he would guess she wasn't going to move till morning.

He climbed into bed behind her and placed a hand on her hip, needing that connection and not even knowing why.

Being mad at her hadn't worked—maybe losing themselves in the electrical connection they shared was the answer? Perhaps they could get it out of their systems while they were stuck here together. But *then* what did he do with her?

He sighed, his brain knotting around the unsolvable problem of Cassandra.

Whatever.

Tomorrow would be soon enough to figure

out what the heck was going on here. And what the heck he was supposed to do about her.

But, for tonight, what he needed most of all was the sleep he'd been denied.

'Dim lights,' he murmured, burying his face in the citrus-scented puff of hair peeping out of the throw. 'Stop,' he added, leaving a slight glow to prevent plunging the room into total darkness. Just in case.

Letting his hand drift over her curves, he anchored her safely to him, then dropped into a deep dreamless sleep.

CHAPTER NINE

CASSIE'S EYELIDS FLUTTERED open the next morning. Her body was rested, her stomach grumbling loudly, but when she moved she felt the tug of yearning, and a slight discomfort between her thighs.

Cocooned in a blanket, it took her a moment to register the blaze of mid-morning sunlight coming through the signature windows she recalled from three—no, four mornings ago, opposite the bed.

The scent of sea salt, wood resin and pine soap had her letting out a cautious breath.

She was back in Luke Broussard's bed— which had to be why she'd slept so peacefully.

She rolled over, scared to look. But the bed beside her was empty, the room quiet except for the accelerated sound of her own breathing. She stifled the foolish sting of disappointment.

The events of last night came tumbling back in fits and starts—the stark shock of Luke's presence in the kitchen, the crippling fear brought on by the power cut, the humiliation of how she'd clung to him in the darkness and then... His mocking smile, her bold challenge... The panic when she'd nearly revealed the truth about her virginity... And then the sex—raw, desperate, frantic, mind-blowing...

But that was all she remembered.

How had she ended up in Luke's room?

She wriggled off the bed, keeping the blanket wrapped around her naked body, and shuffled towards the bedroom door, surprised at how rested she felt. More energised and clear-eyed than she could remember feeling since she'd landed in San Francisco and this whole disaster had begun.

She crossed the spacious room, her bare toes sinking into the thick pile carpet. But then she spotted a thick white sock, neatly folded on the dresser. Shrugging off the blanket, she reached out to stroke the wool.

It was one of the pair she'd been wearing yesterday. Had Luke taken it off her after carrying her upstairs?

A strange choking feeling constricted her throat. She swallowed convulsively and lifted her hand, bundling herself securely back in the blanket.

It's just a sock.

At least they hadn't made love after he'd brought her up here, because that would be even more humiliating. She was pretty sure she'd jumped him downstairs. Although he certainly hadn't objected.

But why had he brought her to his room instead of hers?

She shook off the unhelpful question and opened the bedroom door to peek out. Whatever the reason, she did not want him to catch her in here now.

The buttery, syrupy smell coming from downstairs had the rumbling in her empty stomach turning to insistent growls.

Pancakes? Is he trying to torture me?

Tiptoeing to her own room, she headed straight into the en suite bathroom, dropped the blanket and darted into the shower.

She scrubbed the scent of him off her skin. She needed to get past the memories of last night, erase them from her consciousness before she confronted him and tried to make some sense of what she'd done… What *they'd* done… *Again…*

And figure out how on earth she was supposed to deal with it.

Ten minutes later, she made her way down the open staircase. The buttery aroma was almost as tantalising as the sight of Luke in baggy sweats and an old MIT T-shirt, busy flipping pancakes like a pro.

His head rose and his gaze locked on hers. 'Hey,' he said, his voice as raw as she suddenly felt.

She wrapped her arms around her midriff, thankful for his housekeeper's jeans and baggy sweater. She pressed a hand to her damp hair in a foolish moment of vanity, then dropped it.

'Hi,' she managed round the thickness in her throat.

And to think she'd thought their first morning-after had been the most awkward moment in her life... *Hello, awkward* times a thousand.

He switched off the heat under the pan and slid the pancake he'd been cooking onto the pile warming on the hot plate. 'Grab a seat,' he said, nodding at the breakfast bar.

And she noticed the neatly prepared place-settings—knives, forks, plates, rolled napkins, glasses of orange juice, butter on a dish and a bottle of maple syrup.

Had he been waiting for her to wake up? Had he cooked breakfast especially for her? Why did the thought make the boulder in her throat swell to asteroid proportions?

Luke Broussard as an angry, demanding jerk was manageable.

Luke Broussard as a good guy was catastrophic.

'Thank you,' she managed, as she perched on one of the stools.

With the sizzle of frying pancakes no longer filling the silence he had to be able to hear her stomach—which was so empty it was practically inside out—doing its best mountain lion impression, but he didn't comment as he brought the loaded plate to the table.

'I'm famished,' she said, just to make him aware that she appreciated the effort.

'Yeah, I can tell,' he said, the rueful quirk of his mouth doing nothing to mitigate her embarrassment.

Hadn't she devoured those firm, sensual lips last night, like a starving woman?

That would be a yes.

He served himself a stack of expertly cooked pancakes, added a slab of butter, then doused them in a lake of syrup. 'Dig in before they get cold,' he prompted.

She didn't need any more encouragement.

At least if they were eating she wouldn't have to speak… Which was good, because she still did not have a single clue what to say about last night.

She concentrated on helping herself to three

pancakes, swirling syrup over every inch of them, then slicing off a hefty triangle.

A low moan escaped her as the sinfully delicious combination of fluffy pancake, salty butter and sugary syrup melted in her mouth.

'Bon?' he asked, the quirk of his lips now a definite smile.

She nodded enthusiastically. 'Delicious,' she said, then covered her mouth, which was still full of pancake.

He gave a low chuckle and she set about demolishing her stack and filling the empty void in her stomach.

Five minutes later she placed her knife and fork across her plate, her belly so full she was surprised it hadn't burst. She raised her gaze to find him watching her. He was leaning back on his stool, his empty plate in front of him. Apparently he'd finished a while ago.

The colour leapt into her cheeks on cue.

Yo, awkward—how about company?

'Sorry, you must think I'm an absolute pig,' she said.

His eyebrow quirked, but then he smiled. One of those lazy, easy-going smiles that filled his emerald gaze with heat and approval. She recognised that smile because it was exactly the same smile he'd treated her to so many times on their first night—accepting, appreciative, impressed, aroused—before their first morning-after.

She swallowed, brutally aware of the effect that smile could still have on her as the warm glow—rich and full and misguided—shimmered right down to her toes.

'Come here,' he said, his gaze drifting to her mouth as he beckoned her towards him with his index finger.

She leant forward without thinking, and he glided his fingertip under her bottom lip.

She let out a small, shocked gasp and pulled back, but it was already too late. The light, fleeting touch brought with it a barrage of sensations.

His devastating smile widened as he brought his fingertip to his own lips and licked off the errant drop of syrup he'd captured.

The jolt of awareness in her too-full stomach became a lightning bolt.

'I'll clear up,' she said, lifting the two plates, suddenly frantic to find something—*anything*—to dispel the sexual tension building again at breakneck speed.

His hand clamped on her wrist, sending a lightning bolt deep into her abdomen. 'Leave them,' he said.

'But it's only fair…' she began to babble, trying not to notice the sizzle of sensation where his thumb stroked her wrist. Could he feel her pulse going haywire? 'If you cooked, I should—'

'You can do them later,' he interrupted, the smile disappearing. 'First we need to talk.'

He released her wrist, and the reprieve made her light-headed. *Talk?* He only wanted to talk. Surely she could handle that without bursting into flames... Or begging...

She sank back onto her stool, grateful for the granite breakfast bar between them, and let go of the plates. She dropped her hands to her lap, just in case he could see her pulse still going nuts.

'What do you want to talk about?' she asked with as much guilelessness as she could muster, while frantically rubbing the spot on her wrist where his touch still burned.

He frowned. 'You know what,' he said, pinning her with that intense gaze which had always had the ability to slice right through all her denials. And all her defences. Not that she'd ever really had any with him.

'It shouldn't have happened...' she said, her frantic pulse almost as insistent as the look on his face. Because what else could she say?

'*What* shouldn't have happened?' he asked.

'You know what.' She threw his words back at him, feeling the pancakes starting to dance in her stomach as her pulse continued to jiggle and jive.

'No, actually, I don't,' he said. 'Are we talking about when you came apart in my arms when the lights cut out, or when you came apart after they came back on again?'

She stared at him, quite sure her cheeks were so bright now they were probably visible in San Francisco. Was he actually for real, or was he just trying to ram his point home? That she'd been a basket case last night in more ways than one?

'It's a serious question,' he said.

Fabulous, so now he's a mind-reader, too.

'Both, I suppose,' she said, giving him the only serious answer she had. 'If you want me to apologise again for my behaviour, I will.'

Although she didn't feel apologetic. She just felt… Pathetic. The way she always had as a child, looking for the approval she was never going to get.

But with Luke she'd taken that sad, desperate streak one step further and added hot sex to the mix.

Way to go, Cassie. You really know how to make yourself feel like a total loser.

He didn't say anything, just continued to study her with that steady, inquisitive gaze.

She popped off the stool and reached for the

dirty plates again. 'I'll do the dishes,' she said, fairly sure their 'talk' was over.

'Sit down,' he said, before she could pick up the plates.

She plopped her bottom back on the stool, obeying him without question, and then wanted to kick herself for being such a doormat.

But then she spotted the shadows in his eyes and the pancakes flipped over in her stomach.

Was that pity? The same pity she'd seen last night? She tried not to let it humiliate her. But somehow she knew she deserved it. She'd lost her cool last night, exposed herself to ridicule and worse, and then tried to regain some semblance of control by igniting the explosive chemistry they shared.

She owed him an explanation...

She just didn't want to give him one.

'I really am sorry,' she said.

'Cassandra,' he replied, his tone firm enough to make her gaze shoot to his. 'What the hell makes you think I want an apology? For any of it?'

Luke watched conflicting emotions march across Cassandra's expression in quick succession—surprise, guilt, shame, caution, confusion—and wondered how he could ever have mistaken her for a spy.

The woman was an open book. Even when she wanted to, she couldn't hide what she felt or thought.

But what should have pleased him and re-assured him only disturbed him more. He shouldn't have taken what she'd offered last night, and he sure as hell shouldn't have carried her up to his bedroom and slept with her in his arms the entire night, acutely aware of every shift, every sigh, every moan.

Where had the desire to protect her come from?

She wasn't his responsibility, and certainly wasn't his problem.

But they'd both crossed a line last night that couldn't be uncrossed. And the worst thing was he was pretty sure he didn't even *want* to un-cross it any more.

He'd set a number of precedents with Cas-sandra, right from the first moment he'd met her—maybe even before that. When he'd spot-ted her standing on the other side of the arbour at the wedding party in that stunning dress and been captivated.

Wanting her was one thing—he'd desired women before her. Maybe not with quite the same level of passion and urgency, or the same staggeringly intense results, but when had he lost sight of an objective so easily before?

He never brought dates to the island. This was his sanctuary, his safe place, but he'd brought *her* here after knowing her for precisely an hour.

And, what was worse, once he'd believed her capable of industrial espionage, instead of getting her out of here by whatever means necessary, he'd made all sorts of excuses to allow her to stay. He'd used reasoning he could see now was deeply flawed, because what he'd really been doing was encouraging an intimacy he'd believed himself immune from.

But he didn't feel immune. Not now. Not after last night.

She'd got to him. Not only as she'd clung to him in fear and then passion, but before that— when he'd spotted her watching him in the cove and a part of him had wanted her to look her fill.

Having her stay here any longer was fraught with all sorts of dangers. Dangers he needed to guard against. He'd been dumb thinking he could indulge himself, indulge her, and not worry about the consequences. Letting her get any closer would be a mistake.

'I feel like an absolute fool,' she said, her voice breaking on the words. 'I'm glad you don't require an apology, but that doesn't make what happened any less…' She huffed out a breath. 'Mortifying.'

The emotion he'd been keeping a tight rein

on swelled in his chest, making his ribs ache, but he was ready for it this time.

She'd always been able to captivate him with her candour—even when he'd wanted to doubt her, he'd struggled to doubt that—but maybe it was time to use her transparency to his advantage, and finally get answers to the questions which had tortured him every time she'd stirred during the night.

'Do you know where it came from?' he asked. 'Your phobia?'

She glanced up, her eyes widening. 'It's not a phobia. That's… That's ridiculous. I just don't like the dark. And it was exceptionally dark. Living in London, I'm not used to that.'

It was the same excuse she'd given him last night. He could have left it at that, let her get away with the lie. But the feel of her collapsed in his arms, clinging, scared, not herself, was still far too fresh. He hated thinking of her like that, vulnerable and afraid, because it reminded him of demons from his own childhood.

'Cassandra, you went totally to pieces,' he said. 'That's not you. You're tough. But even strong people have no control over irrational fear if it's the result of trauma. I know. When I—' He stopped abruptly, clamped his mouth shut, then thrust his fingers through his hair, shocked that he'd almost shared something he'd kept secret for so long.

This was about Cassandra—not him. And while he might trust her more than he had yesterday, he wasn't dumb enough to trust anyone that much.

Luckily, she seemed too lost in her own misery to have noticed his slip.

'If that's not a phobia, I don't know what is…' he finished.

She continued to stare at her fingers, clasped tightly in her lap. But finally she nodded. 'I suppose I never thought of it like that, but I guess you're right,' she said, so softly he almost didn't hear her. 'I always thought I had a handle on it, that I could manage it. It's humiliating to realise it was just waiting to hijack me all this time.'

The honest, forthright statement, the admission of weakness, of doubt, and the bravery required for her to speak about it aloud, had his heart swelling to press against his larynx.

He swallowed. Forced the feeling back where it belonged. Mostly…

'So you *do* know what caused it?' he asked carefully, not sure any more if he should be taking this route, but unable to stop himself now.

She nodded again, then met his gaze, her rich caramel eyes so open and candid and her expression so frank and yet defenceless it made his heartbeat slow to a crawl.

'The night my mother died…'

He watched her throat contract sharply as she swallowed.

'I lied when I said I don't remember her. But what I do remember isn't much. I was only four. And she was ill for a long time. My nanny used to take me in to see her. I used to love lying on the bed beside her, just listening to her voice. It was so calm. So full of love, I suppose. But as she got sicker her smell changed, and she couldn't speak any more. I hated that smell—chemicals and sickness and a too-sweet scent which I realised years later was morphine. That last night…' She hesitated. 'The night she died… The room was shadowy and dark and scary. I didn't want to sit with her. She wasn't my mummy any more. I cried. I don't think she knew what was happening…'

She coughed, and he could hear the sandpaper in her throat.

'Gosh, I hope she didn't know. But my father was very angry with me. He called me weak. Pathetic.'

'You were just a little kid—what the heck did he expect?' Luke said, his anger for that small child blindsiding him.

She looked up, her gaze dazed and unfocussed, lost in memory. 'He was grieving. I don't blame him. After that night…after she was gone… I couldn't sleep unless I had a light on in my room. I knew how much he disapproved.'

Her father was clearly almost as much of a bastard as Gino Leprince. But Luke forced himself not to make the comparison. He'd already let too much slip. Anyhow, his father's crimes, his own past, weren't relevant to her trauma. And they sure as heck weren't going to make this thing between them—whatever it was— any less disturbing.

She pressed a hand to her hair, pushing the damp strands behind her ear, drawing his gaze to her clear skin. The lack of make-up made her look so young and vulnerable.

He clenched his fingers until the knuckles whitened, trying to resist the urge to capture her chin in the palm of his hand and kiss the lips he had feasted on the night before.

Things had got way too serious, way too fast. It was time for some damage limitation. He didn't know what he'd expected to happen when he'd quizzed her about her phobia. But it hadn't been the terrifying feeling of connection that was now all but choking him.

She'd been open with him; it was time he was open with her in return.

'Listen, Cassandra… The Wi-Fi signal returned this morning. I'm staying here for another five days on vacation and flying back to the city on Saturday. But if you need to leave I can call you a water taxi back to the mainland today.'

'If you need to leave...'

Luke's offer was such a shock it took Cassie several pregnant moments to process it...and her knee-jerk reaction. *But I don't want to go. I want to stay here, with you.*

Which was totally insane. Of course she should leave. He was offering her a way out of the predicament which had caused her so much anxiety since Saturday morning.

If she left now she would be able to do a much more comprehensive report for Temple—after all that was the only reason she was even in the US. But she couldn't seem to concentrate on her responsibilities to Temple Corp. All she could focus on was the deep yearning that had nothing whatsoever to do with her career and everything to do with the unreadable expression on Luke's face as he waited for her answer.

And that was the weirdest thing of all...

Her career had always been such a huge part of who she was. It was the one thing—the *only* thing, really—that had ever made her feel entirely whole. She'd devoted so much of her life to it. Not just to prove to her father she had value, but to prove it to herself. And she'd sacrificed so much to get where she was now, in a trusted executive position at Temple Corp which had the potential to be so much more.

She'd risked it all four nights ago for one night of pleasure. And she'd berated herself for that catastrophic mistake every night since. She never compromised her career; she always did the best possible job she could. And this assignment was important. To Temple and to her.

But as she sat on the stool in Luke's kitchen, her stomach weighed down by the pancakes he'd made her, his face an unreadable mask, just one thing he'd said to her—unbidden and unexpected—as he'd asked about her phobia reeled through her head.

'You're tough.'

And what that meant.

You have value.

It was the one thing no other man had ever said to her. Not even her father. Because no man had ever known her as well as this man had come to know her after only a few days.

And with that realisation came the knowledge that all her hard work—all the late nights, the missed weekends, the lost friendships, the dedication to her job above everything else which had minimised her personal life—didn't seem worth as much any more as it always had, because of one crucial reality that had only become clear in the last three days.

While trying to impress her father and make him realise something Luke had acknowledged without even being asked, she was in danger of *becoming* him. A ruthless workaholic who had nothing in his life outside his job. Maybe she wasn't there yet, because Ash's expansive friendship—the only social connection she'd managed to maintain in the last four years—had added joy and warmth and humour and an adorable flakiness to her life. But she couldn't rely on Ash for ever to stand between her and the threat of turning into the kind of sterile, soulless, embittered person her father had eventually become after her mother's death.

She had to find her own path, her own personal joy. And, while she knew what she had discovered in Luke Broussard's arms last night, and then in his bed, was not going to last, for the first time in as long as she could remember she felt fully alive. Fully engaged. Fully seen.

She didn't want to lose that. Not yet. Not until she had to,

And so she found the courage to say what she really wanted to say.

'I could stay here and check out other investment prospects online until you head back to the city. Unless you really want me to leave today?'

His eyebrows lifted, and she could see he hadn't expected the question. Then his brows flattened, his gaze becoming even more intense as he studied her... And a part of her—a big, empty part of her—immediately wanted to take the suggestion back.

What was she doing?

What if he said no?

How compromised would she feel?

Why was she giving him the power to reject her?

What was she really hoping to achieve by staying?

But before any of those misgivings had a chance to come out of her mouth, or even really queue up in her brain, his lips quirked on one side in that devastating half-smile—so hot, so confident—that she had become completely addicted to, and he said, 'I don't want you to leave today.'

Her heart leapt in her chest.

She didn't have to go. He wanted her to stay. Sort of...

So she gave herself permission to go with her gut again...for the first time since Friday night.

'Then I'd be happy to stay until the weekend, too,' she said. 'If you're okay with that.'

His eyes flashed with something so hot and fierce and possessive she was surprised it didn't burn her.

'I'm more than okay with that...' His smile sharpened as he reached out and hooked her hair behind her ear, the touch light but devastating, and added, 'On one condition. No work while you're here. This is a vacation. And we've got more than enough things we could be doing to occupy the time,' he said, the passion in his gaze making it crystal-clear exactly what those 'things' might entail.

Need throbbed at her core, but somehow she clung to the last remnants of practicality...and professionalism.

'But I have to work on an investment report that doesn't include Broussard Tech for Temple...' She began, but he pressed his finger to her lips to silence her.

'How long have you got before your trip finishes?' he asked.

'Until next Friday,' she said, her breath catching when his finger trailed down her neck to drift across her collarbone. She couldn't think when he was looking at her like that... As if he might jump her at any minute... As if he wanted to do things that would make her moan...

'That's heaps of time. I know some great start-ups ripe for investment. I'll put you in touch with them once we're back in the city. Okay?'

She found herself nodding, still mesmerised by the desire and purpose in his eyes. When had any man ever looked at her with such hunger... such promise?

'Okay...' she managed, because he seemed to require some kind of answer.

'But no talk of Temple or your job for the next five days? Understood?' he murmured, and that caressing finger dipped to circle her nipple through the sweater.

She choked off a sigh as he plucked and played with the turgid peak.

'Understood, Cassandra?' he demanded, still watching, his smile sharpening with devastating intent.

'Yes, absolutely...' she said, not even sure what she was agreeing to any more as need exploded at her core.

'Good girl,' he said. 'We're gonna have a great vacation,' he murmured, lifting his caressing hand to circle her neck and draw her closer. 'As long as you understand, *cher*, that when we leave here it's over.'

It was what she'd assumed—what she'd always known to be true. All he'd done was say what she was already thinking. This connection between them wasn't about love, or anything romantic. It was more prosaic. It was about need, and desire, and maybe—for her—about changing priorities which had held her prisoner for too long. It was about going with her instincts, giving herself permission to live a little… Heck, to live a lot.

But even so, once he'd said it with such finality, she felt a hollow tug in her chest.

She dismissed it. Forced it back where it belonged, in the box marked *This is just a sexual adventure*, and let the hunger reign.

'I know,' she said, so desperate now she could hardly breathe. 'I wouldn't have it any other way.'

'Bien,' he said, then threaded his fingers through her hair and angled her face for his kiss.

Anticipation shimmered down to her core as she grasped his waist. His hot breath skimmed over her cheek and her heart soared.

'Let's take this upstairs,' he murmured. 'Where it belongs.'

She barely had a chance to nod before he'd lifted her into his arms and headed out of the kitchen, leaving their dirty dishes and the last of her sanity behind.

Excitement rushed through her, blasting away the last of her thoughts about anything other than feeding this hunger. She would take this chance. Take everything Luke Broussard had to

offer over the next five days. Not just spectacular no-strings sex, but the chance to indulge in
all the things she'd denied herself for so long.

Freedom, exhilaration, excitement, fun.

But as he marched up the stairs, holding her
in his arms, she couldn't quite ignore the weight
in her chest warning her she was already more
invested in this moment—this man—than she
had any right to be.

CHAPTER TEN

'ON YOUR FEET, Cassandra!' Luke's shouted command carried across the roar of the surf. 'Now.'

Cassie tensed, her tired muscles straining as she leant forward on the board the way he'd instructed her. *You can do this. Get off your knees.*

But her fingers refused to obey her. She had only seconds before the wave would barrel past her and she'd miss her chance.

'Look at me, *cher*. Don't look at the board.'

She raised her gaze to find Luke standing a few hundred feet away, thigh-deep in the water.

The surfing lessons had been her idea—why the heck had she suggested them again…? Oh, yeah, because otherwise she and Luke would never have left the house, or rather his bed, in the last four days.

But still her fingers refused to relinquish their death grip on the board.

I can't do this… I just can't.

'Cassandra, you've got this.'

The words carried over the tumble of water—powerful, provocative, confident. Confident in her. And in her ability to finally get this right.

And as if by magic the inadequacy which had been holding her back all morning finally let go its stranglehold on her body.

There's no pressure here except the pressure you put on yourself.

This wasn't about pleasing Luke. It was about pleasing herself.

The thought was like a light, blasting the last of the doubts out of her brain—and her fingertips.

The tired muscles in her thighs relaxed. She pressed her toes into the board and finally let it go...

Determination surged through her as she rose to a standing position in one fluid movement. Her legs strained, her knees shook, but she stood upright, instinctively assuming the stance Luke had taught her over the past two days—one leg forward, the other back, her arms outstretched to steady herself.

Her body absorbed the kick of power as the board skimmed across the water. The wave broke behind her and the board shot forward.

Suddenly she was flying. And shrieking. Her joy collided with the rush of triumph.

Her knees trembled, but instead of throwing

herself into the sea, this time she adjusted her arms to balance her stance.

Still up...still flying.

Luke shouted and punched the air. 'Way to go, Cassandra. You're surfing.'

She had one blissful moment to absorb the glory of her achievement. It seeped into her soul and made her heart pound as she flew across the water.

This is what living is actually about.

Then the board wobbled and she tipped, sliding into the surf. She went under, swallowing a mouthful of brine. But it didn't matter because she had already achieved the impossible.

Cassandra James—surfer extraordinaire!

Strong arms took hold of her and yanked her up, back into the air. Exhilaration joined the joy charging through her veins as she spluttered.

'You did it, *cher.*'

A broad smile split Luke's features, making her heart race fast enough to win The Grand National.

'Does it still count? Even though I wiped out?' she said, still not quite able to believe she'd actually stood upright and rode the wave.

'Of course it counts,' he said, while he unstrapped the board from her ankle and strapped it to his own wrist. It bounced and bounded be-

tectiveness. Her heart swelled, pushing uncomfortably against her larynx.

'Fair point,' she said.

She stepped back, out of his embrace. Her swollen heart swooped into her stomach and suddenly she was tumbling again—but this time she was in free fall, and she knew there would be no one to catch her.

She rubbed her eyes to stop the stinging. Tried to steady herself again, but her balance was shot even though she was standing on dry land.

The last four days had been amazing. More than amazing. Everything she had wished for and so much more. The sex had been spectacular. Her body was still humming from all the orgasms, some compelling, some searing and seductive, every one of them more intense and unsettling than the last.

But she'd been ready for that, knowing they shared a rare chemistry. What she hadn't been prepared for when she'd made the decision to stay on Luke's island and grab this moment with both hands was how good the time they spent out of bed would become.

She'd discovered a side of Luke and a side to herself that felt like more than just a physical connection.

He'd been so patient, so protective and focussed on her. They hadn't talked again about anything deep or personal, both far too aware of the end date this moment out of their real lives had, but even so she'd discovered something about him that only made him more compelling, more exciting, more...wonderful.

Luke Broussard might think he was a rebel, a loner, an outsider. And he was a man whom she knew had defied all the odds to make such a staggering success out of his life. But underneath all that ruthless determination and ambition he was a born nurturer.

He'd taught her every one of his mother's signature dishes—she now knew how to cook everything from crawfish étouffée to a mean batch of blueberry pancakes. He also had an encyclopaedic knowledge of the local flora and fauna, which he'd been determined to share. After dragging her off on a couple more hikes through the island's interior he'd taught her the difference between a hawk and a raptor, a red alder and an Oregon white oak. His boundless patience and energy had also paid rich dividends when he'd dedicated their final two afternoons in Pirates' Cove to teaching her how to surf.

There had been no judgement, no cutting remarks, no impossible demands, no ultimatums—even though she wasn't the most able student. Instead there had been only encouragement and excitement at her achievements, however meagre.

The stinging in her eyes got worse. She blinked furiously.

Don't you dare cry. It's just the salt water. You have nothing whatsoever to cry about.

He caught her wrist, dragged her fist away from her face. 'Rubbing them will only make it worse,' he murmured.

Leaning down he grabbed the bottle of water from his pack, uncapped it.

'Here, hold steady.' He cupped her chin, tilted her head back and held one of her eyes open, then the other, to douse them with clean water. 'Okay?' he asked, as he handed her a towel to wipe her eyes without re-contaminating them.

'Yes, thanks,' she said, trying to smile as her stomach bottomed out.

What had she done? And how did she take this yearning back? They were flying to San Francisco tomorrow. This moment was almost over.

'Let's head home,' he said, gathering up the surfboards to lock in the container he had at the far end of the beach. 'How about we hit the hot tub, then nuke one of Mrs Mendoza's pot roasts or something?'

'Sounds like a plan.'

She made herself smile as she packed up the rest of their stuff for the kayak journey back around the point. But her swollen heart had already snagged on the word 'home'.

Luke Broussard might be a natural nurturer at heart. But he wasn't hers—could never be hers.

She swallowed past the raw spot forming in her throat. Somehow or other she was going to have to hold it together tonight, because tomorrow she had to return to reality.

'Hey, come here.'

Luke gripped Cassandra's wrist and tugged her into his lap. They'd done some heavy petting in the hot tub, and filled their stomachs with Mrs Mendoza's enchilada bake, but he'd been itching to make love to her again ever since that moment when she'd stood triumphant on the board and a swell of pride had burst in his chest.

But as he cupped her cheek, leaned in for a kiss, she braced her hands against his chest and pushed him back.

'Problem?' he asked, surprised by the edge in his voice.

He didn't pressure women. But he'd got used to her instant response. That spark of hunger, of need, that had become as natural as breathing— for both of them—every time he reached for her.

Her golden eyes searched his face. 'No, it's

just… I'm exhausted. I thought I'd head to bed now. In… In the guest bedroom. I've got a busy day tomorrow,' she added hastily. 'As soon as we get back to the city, I need to check in at the office and start working on my investment report so I can take something tangible back to Temple in a week's time.'

She was babbling, her nerves evident in the way her body was vibrating under his hands. He stroked her waist, far too aware of the need still thrumming through his system and the instant spurt of anger at the mention of her boss.

Her job was important to her. He got that. And he thought he knew why after spending the last week in her company.

Cassandra was sharply intelligent, focussed and loyal. She was also extremely conscientious. He'd noticed that about her after teaching her everything from how to make a gumbo to how to spot the difference between an oystercatcher and a cormorant. She had an adorable way of processing every single instruction as if her life depended on it… He could imagine she made a brilliant executive assistant. Even if he'd generally tried not to think about her relationship with Temple.

But they'd had an agreement. No work on the island. And she'd broken it. He hadn't wanted to mix this…whatever *this* was…with their professional lives.

The truth was, he didn't want to think about her returning to the UK. And to Temple. Up to now it had been easy to lose himself in the sex and the companionship—which had surprised him more as each day passed. But as she shifted, ready to get off his lap, he found his grip tightening on her waist. He knew he didn't want to let her go—wasn't ready to let her go. Not yet.

And, weirdly, he knew it wasn't just because of the sexual connection that had blindsided them both. Sure, that had been diverting—and intensely pleasurable. But what had captivated him more was *her*. Her willingness to try new things, to overcome what he'd begun to realise were some fairly major insecurities. Insecurities he suspected she'd hidden behind a shield of competence and capability.

He already knew her father had been a bastard, but when he'd watched her this afternoon, overcoming her fear of failure as she came shooting towards him on the board, her face a picture of pure and uninhibited joy, he'd known he could easily become addicted to that look.

'I should go to bed…' she said, sounding exasperated, but he could hear the uncertainty she always made such an effort to hide.

'I told you I would help you with the report,' he said.

'I know, but there's still a lot to—'

'How about I introduce you to the start-ups I have in mind in person once we're back in the city? And you can come with me to the product launch Tuesday next,' he added, cutting off her argument. 'Because everyone who is anyone in the tech industry in the US will be there.'

Adrenaline surged as he made the offer off the top of his head and realised that tonight didn't have to be the end. Not yet. Not if she agreed to his proposal.

Why the hell *not* continue this liaison? They'd enjoyed themselves on Sunrise. She wasn't due back in the UK for another week. The product launch was a big deal for Broussard Tech—a chance to take his company to the next level. And, again weirdly, he wanted her by his side for the events he had planned. Not just the launch itself, but the lavish reception afterwards at one of the city's hippest nightclubs.

'But…' She blinked. *'Really?* Are you sure? I… I thought we weren't going to see each other once we got back to San Francisco,' she said, blunt as always.

'That was the plan, but the plan can change.'

He hitched his shoulder. He couldn't let this matter to him—not too much. But even so his gut twisted when she stared back at him and did that lip-chewing thing again, which had always driven him nuts.

'No reason why we shouldn't enjoy the time we have left,' he added, deciding that mixing *this* with his professional interests and hers didn't have to be a bad thing, if it gave them both what they wanted.

Her brow puckered; her thoughts transparent as always. She was torn—he could see that. Torn between taking what she wanted and doing what was right for her boss.

He stifled the prickle of annoyance.

He didn't like Zachary Temple much, even though he'd never even met the guy. And he liked even less having to help the guy out in order to keep Cassandra with him for a while longer. But if Temple wanted to invest in the US tech scene—as long as it didn't mean any involvement in Broussard Tech—he would throw the guy a bone just to have Cassandra where he wanted her for the next week. Until this need had run its course.

'An endorsement from me will give Temple a huge advantage when it comes to getting investment opportunities in Silicon Valley,' he added.

'I… I don't know,' she said, still tugging on her bottom lip—and making him ache.

'What don't you know?' he asked, not quite

able to keep the snap of frustration out of his tone any more. Why was she being so difficult about this? He knew she still wanted him, as much as he wanted her, so what exactly was the issue?

'I'm not sure what Temple will make of it if he finds out I attended the launch as your guest...'

He hadn't invited her as a guest, but as his date. His gut knotted, the snap of frustration becoming something darker and more painful.

He pushed it back. Forced himself not to over-react. This was about her job. She was scared of messing up, of looking unprofessional, be-cause that was the kind of woman she was. This wasn't about him. Or her loyalty to Temple. Not really.

'Hey... It's not that big of a deal,' he said, ignoring the bitter taste in his mouth and the unhappy shaft of memory of all the times he'd been ostracised as a kid, for something he hadn't been able to change and had no control over.

He captured her chin, lifted her gaze to his. He saw uncertainty and concern.

Yeah, so not about you, Broussard.

'This is just a chance to enjoy ourselves for a couple more days,' he said, with a nonchalance he didn't quite feel. 'And ensure you get your job done while we're at it. That's all. But if you want to call it quits tomorrow, when we get back to the city, I'm good with that, too.'

He waited for her reply, and as he watched the emotions cross her face—concern, confusion, and finally conviction—a weird sense of relief overtook his irritation. Her answer really shouldn't matter that much. He wasn't that ostracised kid any more... He didn't need Cassandra to accept him—or validate him.

'I... Okay, I'd like that,' she said, not sounding entirely certain.

But that didn't stop the surge of vindication rising up his chest and making his stomach bounce.

'If you're sure it's not a bother,' she added.

'A *bother*?' He grinned—he couldn't help it. The question was so quintessentially Cassandra, he found it unbearably charming. '*Non, cher,* it's not a bother.'

She smiled. It was a tentative curve of her lips—as if she still wasn't sure, but she was willing to take a chance—both brave and sweet. 'Okay, then. I guess we have a deal.'

His ribs tightened and he had the weirdest thought that if he'd ever had the chance to date Cassandra James in high school, *she* would have acknowledged him the next day in class. No question.

He dismissed the dumb sentiment.

And the burst of pride and exhilaration at the thought of having Cassandra James on his arm at the product launch.

Still just a booty call.

'Cool.' He cradled her cheek, then swept his thumb across her bottom lip to stop her worrying it with her teeth—and driving him the rest of the way out of his mind. 'How about we celebrate?'

He grinned at the flush that lit up her cheeks as she nodded. Damn, but she was adorable when she blushed. He tucked her hair back, pulled her in, then slanted his lips over hers, not able to wait a moment longer to taste her.

She opened for him instinctively and he feasted on the soft sob of pleasure, the gentle sigh of surrender. When they finally parted she looked dazed, arousal darkening her eyes.

'You still want to sleep alone tonight, *cher*?' he asked, glad he could tease her about it now.

She shook her head. 'I never really did.'

His heart punched his ribcage the same way it had that afternoon, when she'd stood shaky but upright and ridden the wave towards him.

He stood, scooping her into his arms and heading up to his bedroom. *Their* bedroom.

Hunger flowed through him like the wave that afternoon—strong, steady, unstoppable—but, best of all, it destroyed all the other emotions in its path.

CHAPTER ELEVEN

'You look spectacular, *cher*.' Luke's arms wrapped around Cassie's waist as he drew her into his embrace. 'It's a good thing this gown gives you a lot more coverage than the last one.'

She huffed out a laugh at the audacious comment. She'd bought the bronze silk creation at a luxury clothing consignment store in the Tenderloin yesterday, while channelling her inner Ashling. She hoped the dress was just as hip as the first, but Luke was right—it was a lot less revealing than the gold dress now tucked into her luggage in need of repair.

'I don't want to have to punch anyone for staring,' he added.

He nuzzled her neck, his lips trailing to her earlobe. Her heartbeat hammered against her throat at the possessive comment—which was pretty much where it had remained for the last three days.

She cleared her throat and tried to smile as

the mirrored reflection of his hot, mocking smile sent a heavy pulse deep into her abdomen. 'Very funny,' she said, sure he was just teasing her.

She stared at the shimmering silk. So much more demure than Ash's dress. The dress that had caused her so much trouble... Although she was afraid this dress wasn't going to make tonight any easier to negotiate.

She should never have agreed to Luke's invitation to extend their affair for another week. Because after four more days with Luke this felt too much like a real relationship. And tonight... Tonight she was already losing her grip on reality. Thanks to the searing gaze making her cheeks burn.

She didn't know what she'd expected, but somehow she hadn't expected Luke to be quite so...attentive.

After flying them back to the city on Saturday morning, he'd had her luggage moved from the hotel to his apartment in the Presidio. Then he'd arranged meetings for her with a string of CEOs from a series of dynamic new start-ups. The information they'd given her was like gold dust for investors, and she knew Temple would be pleased with the report she had been working on while Luke was out of the apartment preparing for the product launch.

She had finally had the chance to speak to Temple yesterday, to update him on her progress. Thank goodness he hadn't seemed remotely fazed when she'd told him Broussard Tech wasn't looking for investment so she was lining up other prospects. The truth was he'd seemed surprisingly preoccupied.

She hoped it had nothing to do with the astonishing message she'd discovered from Ash after switching her phone on again when she'd got back to San Francisco—and her phone charger.

Gwen's still off sick with her back issues. So I'm running errands for Temple.

Seriously? Ash was working for *Temple*? After being so reluctant even to deliver a tuxedo to him a week ago? And managing to screw that up, according to the last time she'd checked in with her friend?

But Cassie hadn't really had time to investigate. Especially as Ash had seemed more than a little evasive about the arrangement when they'd spoken—and more interested in quizzing Cassie about developments with Luke. But as Cassie had no desire to talk about *that* topic, she'd decided not to press Ash on her new temporary job.

She had much bigger things to worry about

right now than whether Ash was going to flake out on Temple again. Such as how she was going to keep her heart from shattering when she had to return to the UK in three days.

The product launch itself that morning had been a spectacular success. But she'd found it increasingly hard to concentrate on business with Luke never far from her side. She'd expected to be anonymous at the launch, one of the many invited guests. But she'd been anything but…

She shifted round. 'Are you sure I should be going to this party tonight?' she asked. 'I haven't told anyone except Ash about…about us. I don't want to seem unprofessional,' she said, knowing she was lying to herself as much as Luke.

She'd crossed that line twelve tumultuous days ago—and keeping their affair a secret had nothing to do with her job and everything to do with keeping her own feelings in check.

'Ashamed to be seen with me?' he asked.

But even though his lips had curved into that confident sensual smile she adored, his eyes had suddenly lost their twinkle of amusement.

'Of course not,' she said instantly, and her heart squeezed at the thought she might have insulted him.

However much being Luke's date might compromise her business reputation—especially when she was forced to explain the situation to Temple—that wasn't the real reason she was struggling.

'I just… I didn't expect for us to be so…' *Right.* She swallowed the word down, tried to unthink it. 'So much like a couple,' she managed.

This relationship wasn't right—it wasn't even real. Not for much longer anyway.

He stared back at her. 'You've got to come. You don't want to waste this dress.'

He pressed his palms into the fabric, letting the shimmering material rasp over her already over-sensitised skin.

'Even if it's gonna be torturing me all night, knowing how much I want to get you out of it,' he added provocatively, skimming a finger over her breast.

Her nipple squeezed into a tight peak from the tantalising caress. She shuddered, enthralled all over again—the way she had been for nearly two weeks now. Every time he touched her, every time he looked at her with that searing approval in his eyes, every time he made her feel more than she'd ever felt before…

He dropped his hand back to her waist and tugged her close to press a kiss to her temple.

'Don't worry,' he said. 'We won't be staying long.'

He clasped her hand and led her out of the penthouse apartment.

'Which is why we need to get there before midnight,' he added as he stabbed the private elevator button. 'So we can leave early.'

She let the familiar hunger surge. His urgency was as intoxicating as the devilish gleam that had returned to his eyes. But it did nothing to cover the frantic beat of her heart, which was still rammed in her throat.

It wasn't until Luke stepped out of the limo at the venue, with her hand still clasped firmly in his, and headed through the barrage of paparazzi to the legendary nightclub hired for the event—three floors of the world's hottest DJs, housed in an iconic nineteen-hundreds redbrick canning factory in Fisherman's Wharf—that she realised her professional reputation was the least of the things she had already lost to Luke Broussard.

And the only person to blame for that was herself.

'Damn, I thought we'd never get out of there.'

Luke spun Cassandra around as they walked back into his apartment. *Finally.* The sun was coming up over the bay through the penthouse's windows as he pressed her lithe body to the glass and placed his mouth on the hammering pulse in her neck.

He wanted her. *Now.* Had been frantic to have her all evening. Dancing with her had been tortuous…feeling her body move in time with his and knowing he couldn't claim her the way he wanted to claim her without getting arrested.

But he'd branded her as his for all the world to see tonight in every other way that counted.

'I haven't told anyone except Ash about us…'

The quiet words she'd spoken earlier ricocheted through his head again, taunting him the way they'd been doing all evening, tying his gut into tight, greasy knots and making his insides hurt.

To hell with that.

She was *his*. And he'd be damned if he'd let her hide that from anyone.

The echo of her words had faded when he'd paraded her in front of the photographers outside the club, when he'd kept her anchored to his side while everyone came up to congratulate him on the launch, when he'd lost himself in the throbbing bass beat of a retro rap anthem and celebrated his success with her in his arms.

But now what she'd said shouted across his consciousness again, as he grasped the dress that had been keeping her from him and yanked it down.

The sound of rending fabric tore through the quiet apartment and she bucked against his hold.

'Luke…' she said, her voice trembling with arousal, and shock. 'Is something wrong?'

'Not any more…' he said, cupping the breast he'd exposed and capturing the swollen nipple in his mouth.

She jerked, her ripe flesh engorging in a rush as he suckled strongly. He lifted his head to watch as he shoved the remnants of silk off her, leaving her naked but for the swatch of lace covering her sex.

'I need you,' he said, palming her sex through the lace.

The desire to own her, which had been building like wildfire all night, ever since she'd challenged him, was turning into a need so fierce it all but consumed him. Wet heat flooded into his hand as he delved beneath the gusset, found the slick nub of her clitoris.

'Tell me you need me, too,' he demanded.

She nodded, her eyes dazed, and yet she was focussed solely on him as he hooked her leg around his waist and fumbled with the zipper of his pants.

His fingers were clumsy, frantic, as he freed his huge erection, ripped away the last barrier between them, and then lifted her to plunge in up to the hilt.

She took him in on a shocked sob.

The penetration was deep, but not deep enough. He needed all of her—every single inch, every single millimetre. Claimed, conquered, branded.

Her head fell back against the glass as he rocked out, thrust back, harder and faster. But still it was not enough. Her first orgasm hit as her sex massaged his, nearly sending him over too, but he held on, held back. He needed more. He needed her total surrender to make this right.

The terrifying realisation barrelled into him as a titanic climax gathered at the base of his spine, more pain than pleasure. Too raw, too desperate. Suddenly he was that boy again. Needing approval, needing validation, needing respect, needing love.

'More,' he groaned. 'Come again, just for me.'

Holding her up with one arm, still thrusting like a mad man, like an insane person, he found the heart of her pleasure, circled the swollen nub with his thumb. She came around him, pulsing hard, the orgasm even more intense than the first, and he yelled and finally let himself shatter too, body and soul, pouring himself into her.

They sank together to the carpet. Her naked limbs were tangled with his. Her face was pressed into his neck, and the shattered gasps of her breathing matched his as he cradled her body.

And knew he'd made her his, the only way he ever could.

Cassie sat on the carpet, struggling to capture her breath and make sense of what had just happened. It had been like a whirlwind. She felt so raw, so...owned. So exhausted.

It was six in the morning and she knew despite everything, despite all her warnings to herself, that she'd fallen hopelessly in love with the man whose head now rested on her shoulder as they both tried to claw back the sanity they'd lost so comprehensively.

This wasn't just sex. Had never been just sex. Not for her.

The sound of her phone buzzing crashed into the terrifying thought. She reached for her bag, suddenly desperate to escape the painful pressure in her chest which had been there for days but was now threatening to crush her ribcage.

She couldn't be in love with Luke. It would force her right back to where she'd been all those years ago. With her self-worth, her security, tied to a man who didn't love her back.

'Hey...' He grasped her wrist as she retrieved the phone from her bag, her fingers trembling. 'You're not taking that,' he said.

It was a command, not a question. And something deep in her heart twisted. She'd let so much of herself go for this man, and none of it made sense any more. She had to leave—had to get out. Before the damage was irreparable.

'I have to. It might be important.'

She eased herself off the floor, grasped the remains of the silk dress which he'd torn off her only moments before, held it to cover her nakedness. Panic at what they had just shared—so urgent, so basic, so uncontrolled—gathered in her gut alongside the need to run before Luke realised the truth.

Her hand shook as she pressed her thumb to the home screen to unlock her phone and read the message from her boss.

I need you. Can you get an early flight back?

She blinked. Temple's text was so out of character it barely registered for a moment. But when it did, she knew she had a way out.

It was cowardly, weak, pitiable—she knew all that—but as she tapped out a reply on her phone, still trembling from the orgasms which had shattered her, the panic controlled her.

This was a fight for survival now. If she stayed another minute, another day, all it would do was crush what was left of her spirit, her independence and her self-respect.

She'd had misgivings about going to the launch as Luke's date—she'd told him that—and he'd introduced her to everyone—including all the people she'd interviewed for her investment report—as if they were properly dating. As if they were a couple.

Had he known how that would make her feel? Had he done it deliberately? Or did he simply not care enough about her to be cautious.

She suspected it was just Luke being Luke—commanding, arrogant, nurturing, but also possessive—but she also knew that he didn't understand how deep her feelings went…how delusional she had become in the last few days. So he had no idea the damage he was doing.

Still holding the torn silk to cover her nakedness, she said, 'I have to book a flight home.'

'What's wrong?' Luke asked, coming up behind her. He placed his hands on her hips to turn her around.

Humiliation washed over her. He was already dressed—all he'd had to do was zip his flies. And she was still naked and shivering, with the afterglow still racking her body, making her want what she couldn't have. Shouldn't need.

He gently cupped her chin to lift her gaze to

his. 'Who's the message from? Has something happened?'

Her heart shattered a little more at the concern in his eyes. He cared about her—just not in the way she had come to care for him. Why did that make it hurt so much more?

'Temple. He needs me,' she said.

The thunderous frown on his face came from nowhere. And when he spoke, the lash of contempt in his voice shocked her.

'You have got to be kidding me! What are you—his lap dog?'

She stiffened, reeling from the unprovoked attack, and from what she could see in his eyes—which wasn't anger so much as…jealousy?

'He's my boss,' she said slowly, feeling exposed and small. 'This is my job. It matters to me.'

'Oh, come on. This isn't about your damn job. He clicks his fingers and suddenly you're hightailing it across an ocean to do his bidding?'

She pressed the torn material to her breast, shaking now… But somehow, from somewhere, she found the courage she needed to cover the hurt and humiliation burning in her gut.

'What are you implying?' she said, her voice surprisingly calm given that everything she knew about him, about herself, was imploding.

'Just tell me one thing—have you slept with him?'

'You bastard,' she said, his accusation slicing through her heart. 'You're the only man I've ever slept with.'

'What?' he asked, his face a picture of shock. 'What did you just say?'

'Nothing—it doesn't matter,' she said, desperate to claw the words back, their truth making her feel so insignificant, so foolish.

'Damn it, Cassie. Was I your first?' he said, as if it mattered to him.

But she could hear the demand in his voice. And she knew that if she admitted the truth it would only make her more lost, more vulnerable, more unequal.

'Tell me the truth,' he said.

She shook her head. She didn't owe him an explanation. Didn't owe him the truth. Because it wouldn't change the real truth. That she'd given him far too much of herself and all the time she had never meant that much to him.

'It isn't important anyway,' she said, wanting desperately to believe it. 'Because you certainly won't be my last.'

He tensed as if she'd struck him. 'Why the hell did you lie about it?' he said.

But when he reached for her arm, she jerked it out of his grasp. 'Don't touch me, Luke,' she said, knowing she had to protect herself now. She couldn't worry about him and his demons, because her own were already consuming her.

'I don't want you to touch me,' she added. 'I'm leaving, and I won't let you stop me.'

She knew she'd hurt him—saw him flinch as he dropped his arm. But she turned, ran into the bedroom and locked the door, before the great gulping sobs could overtake her.

How could she have given so much of herself and been prepared to get so little in return? She'd succumbed to his will all the way along and lost herself in the process. Opened herself up and told him things about herself that had given him a power over her she couldn't get back. And he'd never done the same. He'd remained closed off—in control the whole time.

All that was left to her now was to run away and own the fact that she'd fallen far too easily.

She dropped the torn dress and tugged on other clothing, her silent sobs making her fingers clumsy, her body convulse.

After throwing everything she could reach into her case, she forced herself to open the bedroom door—and found the room empty.

She knew she couldn't survive another confrontation with him, that he'd done her a favour, but the relief she wanted to feel refused to come.

She scribbled a note, to apologise one last time. She hadn't meant to hurt him. But it would be just one more thing to regret of so many.

She managed to hold herself together until

she was sitting in a cab on her way to the airport. But as she booked a flight, and sent a message to Temple to say that she was on her way home, the tears fell unbidden to splash onto the phone. Because London didn't feel like home any more.

The urge to call Ash, to draw her friend into this titanic mess, to lean on her unqualified compassion and solidarity was immense. But she tucked her phone back into her bag as the cab took the exit onto I-80 and the Golden Gate Bridge disappeared in the rear window, her throat still raw from the look on Luke's face the last time she'd seen it.

She didn't deserve Ash's support now…didn't deserve her comfort.

She'd made this mess all by herself… And now she would have to live with it.

CHAPTER TWELVE

'I NEED TO know where Cassandra James is.' Luke stared down the man standing behind the mahogany desk. He'd had to barge past two security guards and an assistant he didn't recognise to get to him.

'Who the hell are you and how the hell did you get into my office?' Zachary Temple glared back at him.

Dressed in a three-piece suit, his height an inch above Luke's own six-foot-three, Cassandra's boss looked as stuck up as Luke had expected. The furious expression on the guy's face would have intimidated Luke once upon a time, when he was a green kid from the wrong side of the tracks, but it didn't bother him now. Not after an eleven-hour flight, a mad dash from the airport and enough fury and frustration and hurt to keep his temper at fever-pitch for the foreseeable future—especially where this arrogant bastard was concerned.

He never should have let Cassandra leave. But he'd needed time and distance to control all the feelings roiling in his gut at what she'd blurted out.

'You're the only man I've ever slept with.'

How much that admission had disturbed him. And the same confusing emotions continued to churn now. Panic, regret, but most of all…terror. Terror that he'd already lost something he hadn't even known he had.

How ironic was it that those same dumb emotions had got him into a load of pointless fights as a kid?

He wanted a chance to explain. To apologise…to see if her admission meant what he thought it meant. But he had to find her first. And the only person standing in his way was this guy.

'Gwen, get in here,' Temple shouted at the woman he'd barged past five seconds ago.

The middle-aged assistant appeared at the door, looking just as concerned as she had a few moments before. 'I'm so sorry, Mr Temple. He said he had an appointment.'

'Like hell he—'

'I'm Luke Broussard of Broussard Tech.' Luke interrupted the man's diatribe as it occurred to him that Temple—despite his three-piece suit and his carefully manicured appearance—looked almost as harassed as Luke felt.

'Terrific,' the guy announced with biting sarcasm as he thrust his fingers through his hair. 'The man who managed to lose me the best executive assistant I've ever had. What are you doing here? Have you come to gloat?'

'What do you mean, "lose you"? Where is Cassandra?' Luke asked, feeling anxiety tightening around his throat. The anxiety which he'd been busy trying to control for over fifteen hours—ever since he'd returned from a walk around the block to cool off and found an empty apartment and Cassandra's note.

I can't stay, Luke. And it has nothing to do with Temple. Or my job.

I lost perspective on what this is...or rather what it was. I let myself believe that it could be more. And that's on me, not you.

In answer to your question, you were my first lover. I shouldn't have lied about that because it gave it much more significance than it deserves.

Please don't feel you owe me anything. You don't.

The note had damned him—because he'd been able to read the pain and humiliation he'd caused in every scrawled word. But at least it had finally forced him to stop and think long enough to figure out a lot of stuff he should have figured out days ago.

The truth of her virginity had shocked him, but more than that it had humbled him. But what had humbled and shocked him more was the fact that she had lied about it. And what had bothered him was *why*.

One thing was for sure—nothing about their situation had ever been simple. What astonished him, though, was the knowledge that he was pretty damn sure he didn't want it to be simple any more.

Right now, though, he felt as if he'd just wiped out on his board and capsized the kayak at the same time. And the only way he knew how to come back up for air was to see her again.

'I expect she's at home,' Temple murmured. 'Being head-hunted by one of my rivals. So thanks for that.'

'She resigned?'

Luke gaped. He couldn't believe it. The guilt that had been riding him for hours took another sharp twist. She loved her job—why had she left it? Was that on him too? Because paparazzi photos from the launch had been all over the press this morning. And after seeing them he'd finally had to acknowledge another home truth.

It had felt *right* to introduce her as his date. He'd *wanted* her on his arm... And it had never just been about getting vindication for that troubled kid who had once been shunned by his whole hometown.

His guilt at the news she had left her job—that this was one more thing he'd robbed her of, as well as her pride and self-respect—was accompanied by something else.

Hope.

If she isn't tied to the UK any more, maybe... just maybe...

The hollow ache in his stomach knotted and the flicker of hope guttered out.

Getting way, way ahead of yourself, buddy.

Opportunism had once been his strong suit, but all it did now was shame him more. He'd given Cassandra nothing of himself, and that had to come first—before anything else. She needed to know why he'd guarded his feelings while exploiting hers. Why he'd taken from her and given nothing back. She needed to know the truth about that kid. The kid he'd thought he'd left behind a lifetime ago but who was still inside him, always ready to fight, but not ready to heal... Until now.

'You need to give me her address,' he said, jettisoning his pride. 'Please, man. I need to talk to her... To explain.'

So much.

Temple looked unmoved. 'What the hell makes you think I'd give you my executive assistant's address? Why should I? Not only is it unethical, but it's also quite possibly illegal. And I really could not care less if—'

'Because...'

I think I might be in love with her... The words echoed in his head, shocking him right down to his core. But he had the peace of mind to hold on to them. He couldn't think about that now. Couldn't contemplate it or it would just terrify him more. And Temple sure as heck wasn't the person to talk to about it.

'Because *what*?' Temple snapped, his impatience clear.

Luke resisted the urge to grip the guy by the throat and force the information out of him. *Just.*

'Because I know why she resigned her position here. You want her back? You need to let me speak to her—so I can explain.'

Like hell was he going to help Temple get Cassandra back in his employ. He didn't like the guy. But if he had to lie to him to get Cassandra's address, he'd do it in a heartbeat.

'And because this is personal,' he said, when Temple still looked unmoved and unconvinced. 'I hurt her and I want to make it right,' he added.

Temple stared at him for the longest time, considering. And then—just when Luke was sure he'd blown it and debased himself in front of the guy for nothing—Temple grabbed a pad and jotted something down.

He ripped the note off the pad and handed it to Luke. 'Take it. But if you hurt her again, in any way, I'll destroy you.'

Luke saluted the man, so grateful he would almost have been willing to kiss him. *Almost.*

He dashed out of the office, past the assistant and the two security guards who had just arrived on the top floor of Temple Corp's offices.

Now all he had to do was figure out what to say to Cassandra to make things right... Or at least not so wrong.

Cassie's head lifted as the loud buzz of the doorbell drilled into her frontal lobe.

Ash? At last. It had to be. She was for ever losing her key.

Cassie had managed to hold off contacting her BFF on the flight back. But when she'd got home to find Ash gone, having left some garbled note about going to a family event in Ireland, and she hadn't answered any of her texts, the last reserves of Cassie's strength had collapsed and she'd been crying ever since.

Sniffing loudly, she wiped her eyes, which

were red raw, and managed to pick her aching body off the couch. She headed down the hall, feeling as if she were walking through a fog. Who knew heart-ache could be so exhausting? This was like having the flu and jet lag and a hangover all at once.

She undid the chain, her bruised and battered heart squeezing. Maybe Ash could make it better? Because crying for twelve hours solid had only made her a wreck.

She opened the door, her sore heart beating painfully, then gasped. 'Luke?'

Was she hallucinating? Surely she had to be.

But then the vision spoke, his husky voice raw with emotion and reaching right down into her soul. 'Cassandra, we need to…'

It was all he managed to get out before the fog cleared, her heart hit warp speed and she tried to slam the door shut.

Too late. He stuck his foot in the gap.

She managed to stop the door hitting him, her terror she might hurt him more devastating than the shot of pain arrowing through her heart.

'Please, I can't…' she said, but he had already eased the door open, stepped into the entrance hall and closed it behind him. She stepped back. 'I can't do this.'

'I know,' he said. 'I'm not here to hurt you again, I promise.'

He looked as if he meant it, but she couldn't seem to focus on his words—only his face. How could this man—less sure of himself now than before, but no less overwhelming—still make her pulse race and her heart leap in her chest?

'Why did you lie to me about being a virgin?' he said.

She could feel her heart collapsing all over again. *Oh, no.* Was that why he was here? Because he thought somehow he owed her something? Hadn't she explained all that in her note?

She could minimise the fact of her virginity again, but that would give the truth too much power. More power than it should ever have possessed.

'Because I didn't want it to be a big deal...' she said, suddenly feeling unbearably weary. Was this another mistake she'd made?

'Even though it was,' he said, so softly she almost didn't hear him. 'And still is.'

'No, it's really not,' she said, needing him to leave now, before she went totally to pieces again.

He cupped her cheek, ran his thumb over the sore skin where her tears had burned. 'You're a terrible liar—you know that, right?'

She forced herself to pull away, even though she still yearned for his touch. This wasn't fair.

How much more was she going to be forced to endure?

'Just because you were my first, it doesn't make this special, or different...' *If only that were true*, she thought miserably. 'I understand that.'

'But it matters to me,' he said, cutting off the anger she wanted to feel at the knees.

'Why?' she said, not even able to muster the energy to be angry with him any more.

His hand sank to her waist and he pulled her close to touch his forehead to hers. He touched her neck. 'Because you trusted me,' he said. 'And I never trusted you.'

'Okay...' she managed—because what else could she say? Her foolish broken heart was beating double-time again.

'You gave me something precious, Cassandra, and I threw it back in your face because of my own insecurities.'

She breathed in, the tightening in her chest almost as painful as the aching pain in her heart. She didn't want to hope, didn't want to believe...

'It's okay, Luke. I know where those insecurities came from,' she said, remembering the few things he'd told her about his past, and all the things she suspected he hadn't told her. 'I understand them. I have a few fairly massive insecurities of my own,' she added.

'Don't let me off the hook,' he said. 'Because I don't deserve it.'

He kissed her eyelids, kissed her cheeks, in an act of worship that staggered her and had her heart swelling in her chest, making her sore ribs ache even more and her breathing uneven. What was actually happening here? Because it felt like more than she could ever have hoped for.

He placed a tender kiss on her lips. But then, just as she let out a small sigh, feeling the hunger still there, despite everything, he drew away and let her go.

Sinking his hands into the pockets of his leather jacket, he took a step back. He dropped his chin to his chest, looking more nervous than she had ever seen him—and yet more open, too.

'You need to know...' He huffed out a breath. 'I didn't tell you the truth either.'

'About what?' she said.

'I told you I didn't remember my old man...'

His gaze met hers, and what she saw in his eyes had her heart thundering into her throat before he looked away again.

'It's not true. He was sent to the pen just after I was born. But he came back when he'd served his time. Just arrived at our trailer one day, out of the blue. I was fifteen, and I already hated him, but she thought...'

His shoulders rose and fell, and the pain in his face when he hesitated seared Cassie's insides.

'My mama…she thought he had come back because he loved her. Because she had never stopped loving him. He beat the crap out of her…'

Luke touched his thumb to the small scar that bisected his eyebrow, the one that she'd wondered about often, and she realised that his mother wasn't the only one who had been hurt.

'And he took the money we'd been saving to put a down payment on a house.'

'Oh, Luke, he sounds like a hideous man…' she murmured.

'He was.' He glanced up, then stared back at his toes. 'But the hell of it was she refused to press charges… Because she didn't want to screw up his parole.'

His head rose again, and his eyes were fierce and unguarded for the first time since she'd known him. She could see it all now. The pain, the regret, the fury and the deep grief—for his mother and for the love she'd had for a man who didn't deserve it.

'I'm so sorry, Luke,' she said, reaching up to cradle his cheek.

She wanted to soothe, wanted to destroy the demons that still lurked in his eyes the way he had destroyed hers. Was this why it had been so important for him not to feel anything? Not to trust her or any feelings he might have for her?

'He sounds like an even bigger bastard than my father,' she added. 'And that's saying something.'

'Ain't that the truth?'

He chuckled. The sound was rough and raw, but still her heart swelled and beat heavily against her ribs.

He gripped her hand, brought her fingers to his lips and kissed the palm. 'But I don't care about him any more, or what he did. Do you know why?'

'No,' she said, her wayward heart beating double-time at the look in his eyes. Not just approval, not just arousal, but so much more.

'Because I finally figured something out. A part of me always blamed her for being a sap, for falling for a guy who didn't love her back. I swore I would never be so dumb. Which was why, when I started falling for you, I did every damn thing I could to try and deny it.'

'*You*... You fell for me?' Her heart slammed into her throat.

'Yeah… I think I started falling the first moment I spotted you at Matt and Remy's wedding. Busy chewing off your lipstick like your life depended on it.'

He rubbed his thumb across her bottom lip

and she realised she was doing it again. 'Really?' she asked, because she couldn't believe it. *Love at first sight was actually a thing?*

'Yeah, really.' He chuckled again. 'Why are you so surprised?'

'Because... But *why* did you?' she said, still not quite able to let go of the fear that had always consumed her as a child. That she wasn't good enough—would never be worthy of love.

He laughed, the sound low and husky this time, and hot enough to warm the last of the cold, empty spaces that still lurked in her heart.

'Well, that's the easy part.' He brushed his thumb across her cheek. 'Because you're smart and cute and loyal and honest—'

'You make me sound like a puppy.' She interrupted, astonished that she could joke with him when her heart had expanded to impossible proportions and got jammed in her throat.

He laughed again. 'And hot as hell,' he added.

'That's better,' she said, euphoria infecting her soul and making her lips lift up in what she was fairly sure was a mile-wide grin. 'Keep going...' she added.

'I love the way you bite your lip when you're nervous, or concentrating, or doing something you're scared to fail at but are determined to try nonetheless. I love your bravery and your boldness and your ingenuity, and how, even though you have a veneer of efficiency and purpose, it really isn't that hard to turn you into mush.'

A laugh burst out, riding the wave of euphoria right out of her mouth. How wonderful, she thought, to realise that so much of what she had considered her weaknesses, were her strengths…to him.

He took her hand, threaded his fingers through hers and tugged her slowly into his arms, until her hands were settled on his waist and she was staring into his eyes.

'And I love that you're gonna forgive me for being a jerk.'

His gaze roamed up to her hair and over her face, the light shining in his eyes for her and only her.

'You weren't a jerk,' she said, touching his cheek. 'You were just cautious.'

'Not any more,' he said, covering her hand, then bringing her fingers to his lips. 'Not with you.'

She blinked, felt the tears threatening again, but this time they were tears of joy.

He wrapped his arms around her, tucked her head under his chin to whisper against her hair. 'I'm sorry I lost you your job…but how would you feel about finding a new one in San Francisco? I have some great contacts. And I know an island that wants you to call it home.'

The giddy beat of her heart hit hyperdrive. She'd only known him two weeks. This was a big step—a huge step—a decision she couldn't make on the spur of the moment. But somehow, as mad as it was, it already felt right.

After all, it would just be another crazy adventure—and she was getting surprisingly good at those.

'I'll consider it,' she said, being coy two weeks too late. Then she leaned back to stare up at him. 'But don't you want to know if I love you too first? Before you ask me to move in with you?'

He shook his head and framed her face with his hands. 'Nuh-uh,' he said, with the confidence she had come to adore. 'I already know you do, *cher.*'

And before she had a chance to be outraged, or indignant, or to dispute the inevitable, he covered her mouth with his lips and sealed the truth with a soul-searing kiss.

* * * * *

Couldn't put One Wild Night with Her Enemy *down? Look out for the next instalment in the Hot Summer Nights with a Billionaire duet,* The Flaw in His Red-Hot Revenge *by Abby Green!*

In the meantime, dive into these other stories by Heidi Rice!

Claimed for the Desert Prince's Heir
My Shocking Monte Carlo Confession
A Forbidden Night with the Housekeeper
The Royal Pregnancy Test
Innocent's Desert Wedding Contract

Available now!